Valley of the Ancients
A Big Zach and Big Jake Adventure

Frank Gawthorne

Copyright © 2015 Frank Gawthorne. This is a work of fiction. Names, characters, places, brands, media, events and incidents are either the product of the author's imagination or are used fictitiously. Any similarities to actual events and persons, living or dead, are purely coincidental. Any trademarks, service marks, product names, named features, artists and bands are assumed to be the property of their respective owners, and are used for reference and without permission. The publication / use of these trademarks is not authorized, associated with, or sponsored by the trademark owners. There is no implied endorsement if any of these terms are used.

All rights reserved. No part of this book may be reproduced or transmitted in any form or by any means, electronic or mechanical, including photocopying, recording or by any information or storage and retrieval system. Without the express written permission of the author, except where permitted by law.

Big Jake the Bouvier des Flandres

Big Jake the Bouvier des Flandres is an actual dog. He can do most of the tricks or techniques The Author writes about in these books. Except some of the more violent actions. He can actually do over 200 different tricks and techniques. He currently resides in Brush Prairie Washington on a small cattle ranch. He is the Authors service animal.

Frank Gorshin

Valley of the Ancients
A Big Zach and Big Jake Adventure

CHAPTER 1

After we said our goodbyes, I left Sam and Carolyn at the restaurant and went back to Efren's Livery.

"Hey there," Big Jake I called. He came bounding around the corner wagging his stump of a tail. "Hi Boy, did you miss me?" I asked.

"Of course he did," Efren said coming up behind. "He lies by the door and keeps watch for you. I'm still gonna get me one of them Boomyehs or Boomerneighs or whatever you call them." I laughed out loud and Big Jake started barking at both of us.

"It's Bouvier," I corrected.

"Efren I need something you may be able to help me with."

"What might that be?" asked Efren.

"I need me a horse."

"Well, ain't that just a hoot? I happen to know where there might be a few for sale," he laughed.

"Not just any horse, Efren," I said, "but one long on stamina, sure footed and with at least a half a brain."

"You know I don't got no lame brained horses around here," cackled Efren. "Well, I don't know which one you would pick, but I know which one Big Jake would pick."

"What do you mean by that?" I said.

"Well, every time you go off and leave him, he's been playing with that stallion I got out back. He's a buckskin, tough as leather and mean as that dog of yours. Won't let nobody near him 'cept me and Big Jake."

"Well then let's take a look see," I said.

We walked out to the corral in the back and I looked at the most muscled horse I had ever seen. He was large by most horse standards, 19 hands high and shiny. His eyes told the story right off. He was too smart for his own good. I walked up to him and he came over snorting and pawing and carrying on like he was the toughest thing since black powder. I put out my hand and he tried to snatch it from my arm. Just then Big Jake came over and he settled right down. He came over and nuzzled him. Big Jake licked his face and then tore out into the corral; that big horse following him around like he was a dog. Big Jake came back and sat by me. Old tough britches came back over and put his head over the fence and I reached out to him again. This time he smelled and sniffed and I reached up to pet his nose. He actually let me. I think he knew Big Jake and I was pards and he calmed way down.

"He's fine," I said, "I'll take him."

Efren's face lit up and I thought he was going to dance around the barn. "That's quite a horse Big Zach," he said. "Maybe too much horse?" Efren cackled.

"Maybe, maybe not," I replied. "It may take me a few days to calm him, but that's my horse. How much you asking for him?"

"Would two hundred be too much?" Efren said.

"Nope," I replied, "two hundred it is."

"You just bought yourself a horse Big Zach," Efren said slapping his knee.

"Good, now I need me a saddle, bridle, saddle bags, a rifle scabbard and a pair of holsters. You got them too?" I asked, joking.

"No and you know I don't you scalawag," Efren said.

"Then you know where a fellow might get those?" I questioned.

"Why sure I do, but I don't think I'm a gonna tell you."

"I'll let you shoot my Colts," I offered.

"Well then, its Baxter's down on Ash Street. When we going shooting?" Efren asked.

"How about tomorrow?"

"Yep, that be good, real good."

"Ok, see you tonight I might be late."

"Ok Big Zach," replied Efren. "See you when I see you."

CHAPTER 2

"Let's go boy," I said to Big Jake and we went in search of Ash Street.

It was a beautiful warm day in St. Louis and we were having a time, just walking down the street. No Indians to shoot at or arrows to dodge. Yep, it was a fine day. We walked for about 10 blocks and finally came to Baxter's leather shop. I opened the door and we walked in.

"Howdy stranger," an old man said. "I be Baxter, who, you be?" he asked holding out his hand.

"Big Zach's the name," I said, shaking his hand.

"And what might that be?" he said, pointing to Big Jake.

"Why, that's Big Jake, the best Indian fighter west of the Mississippi," I replied.

"You don't say. I thought it was a bear when you first walked in. Never seen one like that before, what kind he be?" Baxter enquired.

"He's a Bouvier Des Flandres," I replied.

"He's a bouvi what?" Baxter said.

"Bouvier des Flandres; comes from Belgium."

"You don't say, you don't say. Well, what can I do you for sonny?" he asked.

"I need me a few things. A saddle, bridle, saddle bags, rifle scabbard, canteen, and a pair of holsters for these," I said pulling out the Colts. "Why ain't those Colt Walkers?" he asked.

"Yes sir they are," I replied.

"Go over there and pick out a saddle and bridle. Saddle bags are over there, and well the scabbard and holsters I'll have to make."

"How long to make?' I asked.

"Well, take me a few days," he said, rubbing his chin.

"I need the holsters to be made a little different." I drew him a picture of what I wanted. "I also need a sack so my dog can ride the horse." He looked at me kinda funny and then a light went on.

"Something he can put his back legs in and have his front legs over the back of the horse?"

"Yes," I said.

"I think I can make something," replied Baxter. "Let me think on it and I will have it ready with the other stuff."

"Can you deliver the whole order to Efren's Livery when they're ready?"

"Sure Big Zach, we can do that for you. How do you want to pay?" Baxter asked.

"How about gold, will that do for you?" I asked.

"Yep sonny it sure will."

I paid old Baxter and said to him, "You might need this to make the holsters," and I handed over one of my Colts.

"Make it easier, that's for sure," Baxter chided.

"Nice meeting you Mr. Baxter, look forward to seeing those holsters."

I called Big Jake and we went out the door.

I broke my rifle when we were escaping from the Blackfoot and I needed a new one, so we went up to Adam's Gun shop to see if he had something I could use. I opened the door and the bell chimed. Walking in I could see Adam with somebody in the back and waited for him to come up front.

"One minute Sam I need to see who's here," said Adam.

"Sure," said Sam, "I'll wait."

Adam walked up front and when he saw me a big smile crossed his face.

"Well, well Big Zach Taylor and Big Jake," he said holding out his hand. "You look well and so does Big Jake. Come with me I have someone I want you meet."

I followed Adam back into his workshop and was introduced to the fellow sitting near his bench.

"Big Zach, meet Samuel Colt," he said. Samuel Colt held out his hand and I shook it with enthusiasm.

"So you're Big Zach," he said. "I have heard a lot about you."

"I've heard a lot about you to sir," I said.

Adam broke in and said, "Oh I almost forgot Big Jake."

Samuel looked down and put his hand out toward Big Jake and he lifted his paw. Samuel shook Big Jake's hand and said, "Nice to meet you Big Jake. I've heard a lot about you too."

After the introductions were over Samuel said, "You must be back from your trapping expedition Big Zach. How did you do?"

"The expedition was a great success but I didn't have much to do with it."

"Oh?" replied Samuel.

"When we first got there, I and another trapper were attacked by over twenty Blackfoot Indians. He was killed and I had to run for my life." Samuel's eyebrows lifted and he said, "I see you made it out all right." "Yes but it was touch and go for a few days. These Colts sure helped bring down the odds," I said slapping the one I had left in my sash.

"I'm mighty glad they helped young man," replied Samuel. "I heard the Blackfeet are dangerous Indians."

"Yes they are and they hate me and Big Jake so much they sent a sizable war party to kill us."

I told them the story about our escape and the warrior that limped back into camp; leaving out the Kokopelli and the Valley in the Mist[i].

"So you killed them all but one?" Samuel said.

"Me, Big Jake and the Grizz," I replied with a laugh.

Samuel and Adam laughed along. "That's an incredible story of survival," said Samuel.

"I wouldn't be here if Big Jake wasn't with me. Him and these Colts turned the tables on them."

"Remarkable story," said Adam. "Just remarkable! So Big Zach what's next for you?" Adam asked.

"We're done trapping. I hear in a few years there won't be any demand for beaver anymore anyway. I thought we would take a little trip down to Arizona Territory for a spell. I hear the weather's nice and we could use a break from this cold."

"Yes this weather doe's get a fellow thinking about warmer climates," responded Samuel. "Well friends," he said standing up. "I have a big day tomorrow so I will bid you both farewell, and if you two ever get up my way, stop in and see me. I would be delighted to show you my factory."

"Thanks," I said, and he left.

"So Big Zach, what brings you here today?" asked Adam

"If you remember the story, I broke my rifle on an Indian skull and I'm in need of another. Thought you might have something for me?"

"Well I've got something over here you might be interested in."

He picked up a rifle I had never seen before and handed it to me. "Never seen one of these before," I said. "Who makes it?"

"I did," he replied. "Something I've been tinkering with ever since those Colt Walkers showed up. This rifle fires the same bullet as the Colt and uses the same firing cap. It uses a bit more black powder than the Colt, but is accurate up to a thousand yards. Want to try it out?" he said.

"Sure do," I replied.

"Let's go out back and I'll show you how it works."

We went back to the firing range he had in the back and he showed me how to load the new rifle. I fired it several times and was pretty impressed.

"I like the idea of having one cap and ball for two weapons," I said. "It makes sense not to have to carry around two sets of ammunition. What are you asking for this?" I asked.

"Please take it as my gift Big Zach. Use it and let me know how you like it," Adam said.

"I can't accept this," I said. "You have done too much for me as it is. Let me pay you, I have the money."

"Ok then say fifty dollars."

"Sold," I said, "and fix me up with two thousand caps and balls. Ok to leave this here for a few days and I'll come back by and pick them up?" "Sure Big Zach no problem."

Adam was always just too generous. I said my goodbyes and on my way out I left a hundred dollar bill on his desk.

CHAPTER 3

"Let's go Big Jake," I said. "I'm hungry and you probably are too."

We walked out and turned left going a different way back to Efren's. We had time and I wanted to see more of the city. It was a crisp afternoon, but Big Jake liked it that way. So we strolled down the streets looking in the store windows just relaxing. We rounded a corner and I ran smack into a lady coming out of a dress shop. She dropped her packages and she was about to scold me when she noticed Big Jake.

"Wow," she said, "what an interesting looking dog."

I bent over and picked up her packages. "May I carry these for you? I asked.

"Well ok," she said.

"Pardon me," I said, "my name is Zachariah Taylor and this big black gentleman is Big Jake."

"My name is Annie, Annie Stillwell," she replied. "He's the most beautiful dog I have ever seen."

"He gets that a lot," I replied.

"What kind of dog is he and where do they come from, and how old is he and is he a male?' Annie asked. "Oh I'm so sorry for all the questions, but I am smitten by your dog."

"Its ok we get this everywhere we go. He is rather a rare breed in the United States."

"I'm sorry," she said. "I must be keeping you from something."

"No not at all," I replied, "we were just enjoying a nice walk around town. What about you Miss Annie are we keeping you from something?" I asked.

"Oh no Mister Taylor, I was just closing my shop and heading home." "You own this shop?" I inquired.

"Yes I do, and sometimes I wish I didn't," she said perturbed.

"Well since we caused you to drop your packages and we are both available, what say Big Jake and me walk you home Miss Annie?"

"That would be nice Mister Taylor, but only if you answer my questions about Big Jake."

"It's a deal Miss Annie lead the way."

CHAPTER 4

"Well," she said, "what kind of dog is he?"

"He is a Bouvier des Flandres. He came from Belgium, a little country in Europe, and I am not sure how old he is. I think four or five."

"You don't know his age?" she questioned.

"It's a long story Miss Annie, some time I'll tell you about it."

Just then a man jumped out with a gun and said, "Give me your money mister and get hers too."

I pushed Annie behind me and Big Jake walked on past him.

"I ain't got no money," I said. I gave Big Jake a hand signal to stay.

"Sure you do courting a fine looking lady like that around," he said.

"I will agree she is a fine lady, but I still don't have any money. Tell you what I will do though."

"What's that mister?" he asked.

"I'll let you live today if you put down the gun and be on your way."

"You must think I'm stupid mister. I'm the one holding the gun," he said.

"Yes, but you're out numbered seven to one."

He looked around and said, "I don't see anyone else you tetched in the head?"

I said, "Big Jake watch." He came up behind the man and started growling with his teeth bared. "Don't move," I said. "You move and he'll tear you apart."

He sorta glanced behind him and saw teeth and more teeth. I pulled my pistol and when he looked back I said,

"And here are the other six you were looking for." I cocked the pistol and he froze. "Now let's do this one more time. Put the gun down and be on your way or I turn the dog loose and six of his friends in this pistol."

"No problem mister I was just funning. Call your dog off and I'll leave." "Hand your pistol over butt first." He complied and I told Big Jake to quit and heel. He came over to me and sat by my left side watching the man. "You got a thirty second head start; if I still see you after that I let the dog go. Times wasting mister," I said.

He turned around and ran down the street as fast as he could, turning around once to see if the dog was coming after him. I laughed and bent over to praise Big Jake. "Good boy," I said and he wagged his black stump of a tail. I looked around for Annie and to my surprise she was holding a Derringer in her hand. "Miss Annie its ok he's gone."

"You were awful easy on him," she said. "I would have shot him in the ass."

"He was just a kid Miss Annie."

"Yea a kid with a gun," she replied. "You know about rattlers Mister Taylor?" she asked.

"Yes," I said, "some."

"Did you know when a baby rattler is born he can kill you just as easy as an adult. Some say there venom is even stronger."

I was about to say something when she said, "Come Mister Taylor I live right over there." She pointed to a nice house on the corner and we walked over. "Please come in Mister Taylor and bring Big Jake with you."

We went in and she said, "Go ahead and have seat, I'll put on some coffee."

"That really sounds good," I said.

While she made the coffee I looked around her house. It looked like a museum for Indian objects. The shelves were loaded with all kinds of Indian artifacts; headdresses, arrows, tomahawks, pottery, clothes, arrowheads, bows, and all kinds of sculptures. I was amazed. Where did she get these? I thought to myself. I got up and looked closer at some of the sculptures and I saw my friend from the Valley of the Mist, Kokopelli. He was as I remembered, a skinny little man playing the flute. I picked it up to examine closer when Annie came in with the coffee. I put down Kokopelli and went back over and sat down.

"How do you like your coffee Mister Taylor?' she asked.

"Black is fine Miss Annie." She poured and I looked at her again only this time she was different. She was lovely and very confident. She was tall, maybe five foot ten, long hair and a very sexy body.

"Annie," I asked, "can I ask you a question?"

"Sure," she said.

"Do you always carry a gun?' I asked.

"Yes I do. This town is full of every kind of robber, murderer and thug you could imagine."

"You know Miss Annie I'm liking you more and more."

We sat around for an hour and she told me about her dress shop and having been in town for only a year. I got up and went over the Kokopelli sculpture and asked her where she got it.

"You know what that is Mister Taylor?' she asked.

"Please," I responded, "call me Big Zach, all my friends do."

"I will if you quit calling me Miss Annie. Just plain Annie will do fine.

"Ok," I said, "deal. And to answer your question, I do know what this is. It's called a Kokopelli."

She looked at me and choked on her coffee. "How could you possibly know that Big Zach?"

"Well that's even a longer story, but I know."

"Ok smarty pants what is a Kokopelli?' she asked.

"Kokopelli, he is known as a fertility god, healer, jokester, story teller and a great traveler."

"And what tribes of Indians use Kokopelli's?"

"Several tribes use him but this one is Anasazi," I replied.

She nearly fell off the couch. She got up went over to me and looked me in the eyes. "Big Zach," she said. "There can't be more than a hundred people in the world that know what you just said."

"I guess I'm one hundred and one," I replied smiling.

She reached up and gave me a kiss on the lips. "That's for saving my life."

I blushed a little and kissed her back only this time it was a lot longer. She broke the kiss and fanned her face. "Big Zach you are full of surprises. I must know the story, will you tell me please?" Annie asked. "Only if you let me buy you dinner," I replied.

"I'll do one better and make us a big dinner right here."

Big Jake perked up and she laughed. "Big Jake thinks it a good idea."

"I do too," I answered.

"Come join me in the kitchen and we can talk while I make dinner."

Big Jake and I went into the kitchen and I sat at the table, Big Jake laid where he could watch the room. He was always on guard.

"Big Zach I have a million questions I want to ask you about Big Jake, you, and how you know about Kokopelli."

I interrupted her and said, "Sure Annie, but me first."

"How do you have so many Indian artifacts in your house and where did you get them?'

She smiled and said that they were her fathers. He was a world renowned archeologist. His specialty was Native American culture.

"I have been all over south, central and north America. I use to love going with him. I even went to college and got my degree in archeology. I've been helping him with his work since I was a child."

"Where is he now?' I asked.

"He's dead. Killed by Indians in Arizona Territory five years ago."

"I'm sorry if I brought up bad memories," I said.

"No Big Zach. I loved my father and he died doing what he loved."

"So why are you making dresses if you are an archeologist?" I asked. "When he died I lost interest, and it brought up too many memories. I had some money saved up and a friend of mine got married and was selling her dress shop here, so I thought I'd give it a try. I'm a pretty good seamstress and the life is tranquil, a bit lonely at times, but I make do."

I saw tears in her eyes and went to her. I grabbed her and held her tight kissing her forehead. "You know something Annie" I asked.

"What Big Zach?' she replied.

"You are beautiful when you cry," and I kissed her long and hard on the lips.

When we broke the kiss she smiled and swatted me with a towel.

"Let's eat, and Big Jake too."

Big Jake got up and went over to her wagging his stump of a tail. "You're the most beautiful animal I have ever seen Big Jake," and she got down and hugged him.

CHAPTER 5

We had a wonderful supper and it was dark outside when we finished. "That was just great," I said, "we haven't had a home cooked meal in close to a year. Thank you very much Annie. Big Jake says thank you too."

After we cleaned up I told her we needed to go. She looked at me and said, "Oh no you don't Big Zach," and walked over to me. "I just found you and Big Jake." She looked me in the eyes and said, "Please stay with me tonight. I need you and Big Jake."

I swept her up and carried her into the bedroom. She laughed and kissed me. "Take me to bed Big Zach and make love to me all night."

I kissed her back and said, "Try to stop me."

We got up early and Annie was in a good mood. "Big Zach," she said, "I'm taking the day off so we can spend more time together or am I moving too fast for you?" she asked.

"No Annie you're not. I want to spend all the time I can with you," I replied.

"But..." she said.

"No, buts," I replied, "I'm yours all day to do with what you want to." She laughed and said, "That makes me very happy."

"So show me Big Jake's tricks."

"Ok," I replied and we sat in the living room as I made Big Jake perform. "Big Jake up," I said, and he stood up begging. "Big Jake stand" and he stood for me. "Big Jake shake hands," and I had him shake both for me. "Big Jake down," I asked and he went down. I said, "Big Jake crawl," and he crawled across the floor. "Big Jake play dead," and he lay on his side. I said, "Big Jake over," and he rolled over and got up. I walked up to him and put out my arm and said, "Big Jake tall," and he jumped up on my arm. I stepped back and said, "Big Jake round," and he whirled to the left. I said, "Round again," and he whirled to the right. I said, "Big Jake limp," and he limped across the room. I told him to speak and he let out a powerful bark.

"Wow!" Annie exclaimed, "Such a big bark."

I walked across the room and put out my arm. I said, "Big Jake hup," and he ran and jumped over my arm.

She had a paper on the table I grabbed it and told him to bring. He came over grabbed it and I told him to take it to Annie. He walked over to her and dropped it in her hand. I had him sit and told him to wave goodbye. He picked up his paw and waved it several times. Annie laughed out loud.

"Now for our last trick; Big Jake bow," and he stood and put his head down on his feet.

"That was great," said Annie clapping. "He is so smart. Did you train him yourself Big Zach?" Annie asked.

"Some things he already knew when I got him, but yes most of these tricks and a lot more."

"What do you mean a lot more?"

"He knows over two hundred tricks as you call them, but they are really survival tools."

"So like what else does he do?" she asked.

"Well," I replied, "you already saw him protect yesterday. He can track, scale walls, and a lot of other things I would be all day explaining."

"I am amazed," she said. "I have never seen anything like him. You are wonderful Big Jake," and he came to her wagging his stump of a tail. She got down and hugged and hugged him. He turned and licked her face. "I love you Big Jake."

She walked over to me and said, "I think I love you too Big Zach."

I kissed her and we sat down.

I asked her again about the Kokopelli. "Annie," I said, "where did the Kokopelli come from?"

She looked at me and said, "Why are you so interested in it?"

"Because it may lead me to a place I need to go."

"A bit mysterious aren't you?" she asked.

"Yes, but I have good reason," I replied.

"Ok, if you don't want to talk about it," she replied a little hurt.

"I will tell you why if you answer a few more questions."

"Ok," she said and sat down on the couch. "You look different Big Zach is this something you would rather keep to yourself?"

"No Annie I need to tell someone, but I need to know a few things from you first."

She said, "Ok Big Zach you got my full attention."

"First where did the Kokopelli come from?"

"From a dig In Arizona Territory. An Anasazi dig, maybe ten years ago." "Do you know where?" I asked.

"Yes I was there when father found it."

"How much do you know about the Anasazi? I asked.

"I guess quite a bit. It was my father's favorite culture, he couldn't wait to discover where they had gone and why."

"What if I told you I know where they went and why?"

"Why, how could you know that Big Zach no one knows for sure? There are many speculations on where and why, but they are just that. The Anasazi died out thousands of years ago."

"No they didn't," I said. "I know; I was in their city not five months ago." She sat there stunned. "You have me a little scared Big Zach. What you are saying is impossible. You can't really believe you were with this people?" She looked me in the eye and said, "You do believe you were there like you said."

"Yes and I lived with them for over two months."

"Where Big Zach, and how many were there, what did they look like?" "So do you believe me?"

"Yes Zach I do, but how?"

"One more question please," I asked.

"Ok Big Zach."

"What if I asked you to be my partner on a dig as you called it?"

"Where Zach?" she asked.

"Arizona," I replied. "I don't know how long this will take, but I have to find something there."

"What Big Zach, what do you need to find?" she asked.

I looked her in the eyes and said, "Anasazi Gold."

"You know where it is?" she asked excited.

"No, but I need your answer before I go on."

"Big Zach, something like this could take a few thousand dollars and who knows how long."

"I have the money and a lot more," I replied. "I also have all the time it will take."

"Damn Big Zach, it means selling my store and house, and wow you really think you can find it?"

"Not by myself I can't, but if you go with me I think we both can."

"You really believe this don't you?"

"Yes, and you will too once I tell you how I know."

She got up and walked over to the Kokopelli and picked it up. She looked up and heard her father. "Go Annie find the Anasazi and their gold."

She turned and said, "Yes Big Zach I will go."

CHAPTER 6

For the next several hours I told Annie the whole story from start to finish. I left nothing out. Annie sat on the couch and listened saying nothing. When I finished she looked at me and said, "Unbelievable Big Zach, just unbelievable."

"Yes," I said, "I still can't believe it and I lived through it. So did Big Jake."

She looked down at Big Jake and was silent for a minute. She looked back up at me and said, "When do we leave Big Zach?"

"I was hoping for next week, but we need to plan and provision. Once we do that we can leave, but I have one more thing to show you."

"What Big Zach?" she asked.

I pulled the map from my bag and handed it to her. "This," I said, "is the map Mathew gave me."

She took it and unfolded it on the table. She examined it very closely. "This is an animal hide, probably antelope and it is very old," she commented. "These symbols are definitely Anasazi. You see this symbol here?" she pointed. "It's their symbol for water, and this one here is their symbol for the sun. And these here are Aztec in origin. My father believed their descendants were Aztec. This doesn't prove it, but my god Big Zach, this could be the missing link in their history," she said quite excited. "You see these mountain ranges here and here?" she pointed, "and this long valley. I have been here Big Zach. It's the Valley of the Ancients."

I hugged Annie and looked her in the eyes, "You are beautiful and I think I love you too. We have a lot of planning to do," I said.

"What do you think we will need to take?" I asked Annie.

"Well," she pondered, "we will need a lot of digging equipment, but most of what we need we can buy when we get to Arizona Territory. We'll need camping gear, food and water, warm clothes, writing paper, and guns. The Indians down there can be friendly one minute and kill you the next," she said.

"I saw you have the Derringer, but do you have any other weapons?" I asked Annie.

"No Big Zach I don't."

"No problem I know just where to get you outfitted. I forgot to ask; can you ride a horse?"

"Yes Big Zach, I can ride a horse," she said laughing.

"We have a busy day ahead of us. Let's go and meet a friend of mine. I think he can take care of your shop and house and I trust him. Then we'll go see an old friend and get you a horse. I have another friend who sells guns. We'll see him later if we have time."

We got ready and left to see Mr. Goldman at the bank.

Annie grabbed my arm and said, "Big Zach what have you got me into?" and we laughed. I hailed a handsome cab and he whisked us off to the bank.

When we arrived I paid the cabbie and we walked up the steps. Barney opened the door and said, "Good morning Mr. Taylor and Miss...?"

"Miss Stillwell," I answered.

"I assume you want to see Mr. Goldman today?" he asked.

"Yes, is he in?" I asked.

"Jackson," he barked, "Mr. Taylor and Miss Stillwell to see Mr. Goldman."

"Oh Mr. Taylor," Jackson said, "right this way. I will get Mr. Goldman."

Mr. Goldman came out a few minutes later and said, "How nice to see you Big Zach," shaking my hand. "And who is this lovely young lady?" he asked.

"Miss Stillwell, a friend of mine."

"Good to meet you Miss Stillwell. Won't you both come into my office?"

He ushered us in and closed the door. He went around his desk and said, "Please be seated and tell me how I may help you."

Annie took over and told him a lie that she was moving and needed to sell both her home and her dress shop. He listened and then said he could help her get both sold for a fee. She agreed and they made arrangements for the money to be put into her account. She also said that she needed a place to store her belongings until she came for them.

"I just happen to own a warehouse. You can store them there until you are ready to pick them up."

We both thanked him and got up to leave.

When we went through the bank doors Big Jake bolted down the steps and turned to look at us wagging his stump of a tail.

"Come on boy," I said, "we got some more stops to make."

I hailed another handsome cab and told him to take us to Efren's Livery.

Fifteen minutes later we pulled up and I helped Annie down and paid the cabbie.

"Come with me," I said to Annie. "Don't be too concerned with old Efren, he may drool when he sees you. Efren, you around?" I hollered. "Yes, yes I'm here," he squawked.

When he came into view his eyes got big around and he nearly choked on his tobaccy. "Well I be," he said. "Big Zach and that must the Queen of Sheba?" he asked.

We all laughed and Annie said, "No my name is Annie," and shook his hand.

"Well iffin you ain't the Queen of Sheba you ought to be," he rambled out. We laughed again.

"How's my horse doing Efren?" I asked.

"Just the way you left him, mean and cantankerous."

"Let's show him off to Annie," I said.

"Ok Big Zach, this way."

Big Jake beat everyone to the corral and there he was.

"My word," said Annie, "what a magnificent horse. I don't think I have ever seen one quite that filled out." Just then Big Jake took off running out in his corral and they both ran around having some fun.

"He follows Big Jake around like he was a dog," said Annie. Big Jake came back and sat by my side. "What's his name?" Annie asked.

"Well I just bought him yesterday and ain't thought on it," I replied. "Say Annie you name him," I asked her.

"Ok Big Zach Taylor I will."

The stallion came over to the fence and Annie reached up to him. I was amazed when he let her touch him. She spoke up and said in a loud voice. "The Queen of Sheba has spoken, your name will be Buck from this day forward," and she curtsied. We all started laughing and Buck took off around the corral with Big Jake in pursuit.

"Efren," I asked, "you got a horse for Annie to ride?"

"Sure I got lots of horses, what you looking for Miss Annie?" he remarked.

Right then she looked around and stopped in her tracks. "What is that?" she remarked to Efren.

"That's a horse I just bought this morning," he said. "The owner was going back east and couldn't take him with him."

"What kind is he?" she asked amazed.

"He's a gelded Appaloosa."

"I believe I'm in love," she said under her breath.

The horse was a good 16 hands and the prettiest black and white colors.

"The owner said he could run the ears off a jack rabbit. He also said he was really trained up, but he didn't have time to show me much." "What's his name?" Annie asked excitedly.

"You got me there Miss Annie. I forgot to even ask."

"Is he for sale Efren?" she asked.

"Sure he is ma'am," Efren responded.

"How much Efren?" she asked.

"Well I ain't thought on it Miss Annie."

"I'll give you a hundred dollars more than you paid for him?" she asked.

"Well I don't know Miss Annie he's worth a lot more than that. I'll tell what we'll do. Since yourn a friend of Big Zach's."

"Big Jake too," she reminded him.

"Yes and Big Jake. I'll saddle him and you can ride him. If you like him I'll sell him to you for one hundred fifty over what I paid for him and that young lady is a bargain, he's worth twice that much. I'll even throw in the saddle. You ain't got no riding britches on though."

"Don't you worry about that, get him saddled Efren."

CHAPTER 7

Efren saddle the Appaloosa and Annie jumped aboard dress and all and rode him all around the corral. She finally jumped off and said, "You have a deal Efren," and shook his hand. "I can't pay you until tomorrow though," she said.

I spoke up and said that I would pay for him and she could pay me back later.

"Well Miss Annie what you going to call him?"

She said in loud voice, "The Queen of Sheba speaks again, from this day forward you shall be called Percy."

Efren looked at me and me at him.

"Just kidding gents, just wanted to see if you were both were paying attention. Your name shall be Thunder so says the Queen of Sheba." We all laughed for a quite a while.

I followed Efren into his office and told him we would need another pack horse. He looked at me and said, "She going with you Big Zach?"

"Yes," I said, "she's my new partner." I paid him for Buck, Thunder and the two pack horses. "I got my new saddle and some other things being delivered tomorrow. I'll come by in the afternoon and start getting Buck calmed down."

"Sure Big Zach," Efren said. "See you tomorrow afternoon."

When we left Efren's, me and Big Jake just walked out, Annie floated along with us.

"I'll pay you tomorrow for Thunder Big Jake," Annie said.

"No you won't Annie," I replied. "He's my gift to you for taking such a chance on me and Big Jake."

"You big galoot you're taking just as much a chance on me, but thank you Big Zach. I'll thank you proper later."

"I can't wait I replied."

She smiled back at me.

We made our way to Adam's gun shop and entered the door. The bell chimed and Adam came right out.

"Big Zach," he said offering is hand. "Back so soon."

I shook it and said, "How are you today Adam?"

"Good and you?"

"Very good. Pardon me, this is Miss Annie Stillwell."

"Good to meet you," he said shaking her hand. "Don't you look lovely today?"

She blushed and said, "Thank you."

Just then Samuel Colt came out from the back. "Big Zach good to see you again," he said.

"Mr. Colt, good to see you again too," I replied. "This is Miss Annie Stillwell," I said to Samuel.

"Nice to meet such a lovely young lady."

"What brings you two in today?" Adam asked.

"We need some pistols for the young lady," I replied.

Adam looked at Sam Colt and then they both laughed. "Sorry," said Sam, "but we were just discussing my new pistols and if a lady could shoot them."

"You have something newer than the Colt Walkers?" I asked.

"Yes I do, would you two like to see them?"

"Of course we would!"

They took us back into the Adam's work shop and four of the prettiest pistols lay on the table. "Big Zach these are my newest inventions. The big ones are Colt Dragoons and the smaller ones are Baby Dragoons. The full size shoots the exact cap and ball as the Colt Walker. The Baby Dragoon is a thirty one caliber. Here," he said handing one to me and one to Annie.

I hefted it and it was heavy. "Well young lady what do you think?"

"I really like it," she said. "But is it accurate?"

"Well let's find out."

Adam loaded up both pistols and we followed them back into the firing range. "Ok Miss Annie, you first." She cocked the Baby Dragoon sighted in and fired.

"Bullseye," said Samuel Colt.

"Good shooting young lady," said Adam. "Now shoot the rest Miss Annie."

She sighted in again and fired as fast as she could cock the weapon. They all hit the bullseye except one that just hit the outside of the bullseye.

"Wow," said Samuel Colt, "that was spectacular." Where did learn to shoot young lady?" he asked.

"I have been shooting all my life," she responded. "Some of the places my father took me weren't exactly friendly."

"Well Miss Annie I am impressed," said Samuel Colt.

"Your turn Big Zach," said Adam, "there is a new target."

I cocked the pistol and sighted in, fired, and missed just outside the bullseye. "Shoots a might to the left," I said.

"Shoot the rest," said Sam Colt. I sighted in again and fired all five shots as fast I as I could cock the pistol. All five went into the bullseye. "Good shooting," said Sam Colt. Adam just cheered.

"Well Mr. Colt I am impressed," I said. "This isn't just a pistol it's a hand cannon." Adam and Samuel laughed.

"What about you Miss Annie?" Samuel asked.

"What's not to like Mr. Colt? I'll take both of them," she said.

"Oh my," said Adam, "these are mine to evaluate, but..." he looked at Samuel and back at me. "Big Zach you and the lady going into harm's way?" he asked.

"Yes Indian territory same place Annie's Father was killed, Arizona Territory."

"Adam," said Samuel Colt, "sell them to them and I'll send four more as soon as I get back. Can't have these two brave souls in harm's way without proper protection."

"Ok Sam, I couldn't agree more," said Adam.

"Can I pay you now and we'll come back and pick them up?" I asked. "Sure Big Zach, they'll be here when you want them."

I paid, said our goodbyes and we left for Annie's house. I called a handsome cab and we were dropped off twenty minutes later.

"I famished," said Annie.

"Me and Big Jake could eat a buffalo," I replied.

We went in and both sat on the couch. I reached over and gave Annie a big hug and a kiss. She cooed and said, "Let's play for a while before we eat."

I jumped up and dragged her into her bedroom.

CHAPTER 8

After we had eaten Annie wanted to look at the map again. I pulled it out and we both studied it again hoping to glean anything more from it. "Mathew said to follow Kokopelli," she said patting the drawing on my shirt. "He will lead you to the treasure of the ancients."

"Yes, but what does it mean?" I asked.

"Look here," Annie said. "See the marks here? They lead south, but end at the bottom of the map."

"So what are you saying, we have only half a map?" I asked.

"Maybe," she responded, "but it could mean we only have a section of a larger map. If we find the piece that's connects to the bottom here there may be more after that, but we won't know until we find the other piece of the puzzle. You," said Annie, "asked if they didn't value gold."

"Not where they were they had so much of it."

"So if that's true, what is the treasure they hid?"

"It could still be gold," I said.

"Just because they didn't value it, they knew the Spanish sure did. They killed and plundered many Indian tribes just for their gold. This doesn't make sense," she added. "The conquistadors were long gone before they moved their civilization. So whatever treasure Mathew is talking about wasn't hidden until they decided to leave. It could still be gold," she said. "They prized the mineral for its beauty not its value. When my father and I went to dig the Anasazi ruins we didn't find a trace of gold, but you saw it everywhere in their new home."

"Yes," I replied.

"We know there are rich deposits of gold and silver in Arizona so it still may be gold they hid. Large amounts of gold are very heavy so they wouldn't want to carry it all that way. And besides it was actually worthless to them except for its pleasing look. Did Mathew say anything else you can remember Big Zach?" Annie asked.

"Let me think," I said. "All hell was busting lose and I may have missed something, let me think a minute. Ok, I think I remember exactly what he said. Write this down. 'Big Zach,' he said, 'take this map. When we left our old homes we buried our treasure so no one would find it until we returned. We had no way of bringing it with us.' He coughed and blood came from his mouth. 'I am dying,' he said. 'Take the map and Zerena, leave this place. Save yourselves.' He looked up at us and said 'follow Kokopelli' patting the drawing on my shirt 'he will lead you to the treasure of the ancients.' He thrust the map into my hand and in a dying voice said 'your journey starts here' and he died in Zerena's arms."

"Does that help any?" I asked.

"I'm not sure," replied Annie, "but he said they could not take it with them. So it must have been either too heavy or too much. Maybe we're looking at this all wrong," she said. "Maybe what we should do is try to make a list of what we think they considered valuable. You were among them can you remember anything?" Annie asked.

"Let me think. They valued their corn, but they must have taken it with them because there were fields of it growing there. The only other thing I can think of that was everywhere were the paintings of Kokopelli. They didn't want for a thing, but just because they didn't think of something as being valuable in their new home didn't make it not valuable in their old home."

"Big Zach you were in the palace, was there anything on the walls or in the floor beside gold?"

"No Annie. It was all gold. Annie let me ask you this; did you see any mines around the Anasazi villages?"

"No we didn't, but that doesn't mean they didn't get it from somewhere else. Wait a minute," she said. "Somewhere else! My father and some of his colleagues thought that the Anasazi came to America from Mexico and we know the Aztecs regarded gold very highly, but most of it was taken by the Spanish, and very little has been found since."

"So where does this leave us?" I asked.

"Right back where we started I'm afraid," Annie replied, "but whatever the treasure is, it will be the archeological find of the century. Whoever discovers it will be rich and famous, but I'm not going on the trip to be rich and famous Big Zach, I'm going because you asked me, and my father would have wanted me to find the answers to these ancient people."

"I know Annie," I said. "And I trust you. If it does turn out to be nothing but an archeological find and not valuable, you have my permission to become rich and famous."

Annie laughed. "We won't find the answers here so the sooner we leave the sooner we can solve this mystery." She folded up the map and put it back into my pouch. "Let's call it a night and get some sleep. Maybe tomorrow things might be clearer."

"Sounds good to me I," said yawning.

CHAPTER 9

Tomorrow brought a beautiful sunny day, but it was still cold out. Annie had gone out to arrange getting her things packaged and moved. Me and Big Jake got ready and left for Efren's. I still had some work to do with Buck before we could leave. Annie said that she would meet us there in the afternoon.

On the way there we stopped and picked up our guns. Adam put them in a big bag and I told him somewhere down the line we'd meet again. "Good luck," he told me, and we left for Efren's.

When we arrived at Efren's he was looking at my new saddle.

"Well old timer," I said, "does it meet with your approval?"

"Hi Big Zach these just arrived. And yes, old Baxter knows how to make a saddle. Here are some other things."

"My holsters," I said. "Let me try them on."

They fit perfectly so I went into the bag and brought out my new Colt Dragoons. My Colt was a bit snug, but that was just fine. When they broke in they would fit better. I put the other Colt in the other side and tried to draw them out real fast. It was slow, but I could practice on our way to Arizona Territory. I went and got the box the Walkers came in and put them back inside.

"Hey Efren, I got a present for you."

He came over and said, "What you got there?"

I handed him the Colts and he just looked at me. "What do you mean by this?" he said, "don't you need 'em?"

"Nope not anymore," I said back to him. "I bought two new models from Samuel Colt. Want to see them?"

"I sure do!" he said.

I pulled them out of my holsters and showed them to him. "Here," I said, "look at these. There Samuel Colts newest invention. He calls them Colt Dragoons," and I gave one to Efren.

"My word," he said, "these are heavy aren't they?"

"Yes," I said, "and they are damn accurate. They shoot the same bullet as the Walkers do and they are made a lot better."

I took off the holster and went to see Buck. He was as rangy as ever and I whistled to him. He came over and I gave him a piece of sugar. He liked it a lot and then took off around the corral. I whistled again and he came back over to me. I gave him another piece of sugar and I saw a light go on his eyes. Whistle, sugar. So I left and went back to the saddle and got it ready. I came back a few minutes later and whistled again. He raced over to me. I gave him another piece of sugar only this time I caught his halter and rubbed him on his chest and sides. He seemed to like it. I let him go and he raced around the corral again and I left.

I grabbed the saddle, blanket and new bridle and put them on the ground beside me. I whistled again and he came running. I gave him the sugar and caught the halter again. I removed it and put on the bridle. He was a little skittish at first, but settled right down. I gave him another piece of sugar and climbed in with him. He backed up a little and then came back looking for more sugar. I grabbed up the blanket and let him smell it for a minute and laid it on his back. I saw old Efren looking on from the door with Big Jake by his side. I gave him another piece of sugar and grabbed the saddle, let him smell it for a second and put it on him. He backed up again, but settled right down when I talked to him.

"Good boy Buck," I kept repeating, and cinched up the saddle. I grabbed the reins and took him for a walk around the corral several times. I brought him back to the fence and whistled again; he whinnied and I gave him another piece of sugar. It was now or never so I moved along side of him. "Whoa boy, whoa boy," and I got up on him.

He backed up and started to buck a little as I rode him around the corral. "Efren," I said, "open up the gate."

He came over threw open the gate and backed away. I rode him around the corral several more times and then out the gate we went. He tore down the road out of town and I just let him have his head. It had been a while since he had run.

I looked back and Big Jake was following, but he was getting left behind. I pulled on the reins and told Buck to calm down. After a few more minutes he settled down and I pulled him to a stop. Big Jake caught up with us a few minutes later and Buck bent over to see him. Big Jake licked his face and we headed back to Efren's at a walk. This old boy could run, but I still needed to see if he could be controlled.

I went through the turns and stops and tried to get him to back up. He knew what to do and I could tell old Efren had put a lot of time in on him. I put down the reins and used my knees to control him, he answered every command. I was thoroughly impressed and I meant to tell Efren just that. We walked back into the corral and I got off, removed the saddle and blanket and put his halter back on. I let him go and he raced around the corral.

I whistled and he came over to me. I rubbed him and then gave him the sugar.

I took the saddle back inside and clapped Efren on his back.

"You did a fine job with that horse," I said, "he is one well trained horse."

"You did pretty good with that sugar trick your own self," he replied. "Something an old mountain man showed me a while back."

"Efren, Big Zach, you here?" I heard Annie call.

Big Jake raced out front and brought her back.

"Hi boys how's Buck and Thunder today?" she asked.

"Big Zach here just got back from taking Buck out. Did fine, real fine. Show her the new trick you taught him," said Efren.

"Ok," I said and whistled. Buck came running over and I rubbed on him and gave him the sugar.

"You did that in one day?" she asked impressed.

"Yep he's a smart horse and wants to please," I said. "You get done what you needed?" I asked.

"Yes and we're all set."

"Ok then we need to get our gear in order and tomorrow we'll take both horses out for a long run. We should be ready to leave in a couple of days."

"Suits me," Annie said. "How long to get to Arizona Territory you figure Big Zach?"

"May take a month or more, but it will give us both time to get acquainted." I winked. "I got your guns so I thought tonight we'd get familiar with them and get you a holster tomorrow. Well Efren we're off to Annie's see you in the morning."

"Ok you two," he said, "see you tomorrow."

"Let's go Big Jake," I called, and we left for Annie's.

CHAPTER 10

"Annie," I said, "we still have some time left, let's do a little shopping. There's a ships store down the street I want to visit."

"Ships store?" she asked.

"Yes I want to get one of those sailor telescopes and some rope."

I hailed a cabbie and a few minutes later we arrived at the ships store. "Wait for us please," I asked the cabbie and he nodded his head.

We went in and the clerk said, "What an interesting dog you have. I have never seen one like it. He is very, well... hairy" he said. "What breed is he?"

"He's a Bouvier des Flandres," Annie said proudly, "and they come from Belgium."

"Amazing looking animal," he commented. "What can I do for you two today?" he asked.

"I need me one of those sailor telescopes," I said.

"Then please come over here, we have them in this case."

I picked out one I could put in my pouch. "Here," the clerk said and handed me the telescope.

I opened it up and looked through the eye piece. "Annie," I said, "you look so small."

The clerk said, "Sir you're looking through the wrong end."

I turned it around looking a bit embarrassed. I looked again and took it from my eye and looked again. "Wow, these really bring things up close," I said. I handed it to Annie and she tried it.

"It really is very clear."

"We'll take it," I said, "and five hundred feet of that rope there."

I paid the clerk and we headed back to Annie's.

Annie played with the telescope all the way to her house. Twenty minutes later we arrived and I paid the cabbie.

We sat at the kitchen table and I put our guns on a piece of paper. I showed Annie how to disassemble them and how to clean them. She figured it out pretty fast.

"So," I said, "let's see who can take them apart and put them back together the fastest."

Annie liked the competition and said, "Ok Big Zach, loser does the dishes tonight."

I said, "Ready, set, go," and we went to work.

I was having a little trouble getting mine apart and looked over to Annie who was already putting hers back together. She said, "Done," and I came in a close second.

"Looks like you're doing the dishes tonight."

I smiled and said, "Beginners luck."

She laughed and said, "Better lucky than good."

We both loaded up the pistols and put them away.

"Big Zach," Annie said, "let's have another look at the map."

I retrieved it from my pouch and unfolded it on the table. She looked at it for several minutes and looked at me. She picked up the piece of paper she had written Mathew's dying words on, and read a line. "He thrust the map into my hand and in a dying voice said your journey starts here. I think what we have here is a map of just what Mathew said, a starting place. A place for whoever had the map to start their journey to find the treasure. So we already know where this is."

"The Valley of the Ancients," I said.

"Yes," she replied. She looked back at the map and asked me to bring the Kokopelli from the shelf. I handed it to her and she compared the two. "Look," she said, "these are different. The one on the map is playing a small flute and has a hump on his back. This one," she said, "has no hump and is playing a long flute. Big Zach," she said excited, "when I was in the valley with my father he asked me to copy all the petroglyphs. There wasn't all that many, but I think I still have them." She got up and rushed to her room. A few minutes later she returned and gave me half the stack of drawings.

"See if you can find one that matches the one on the map."

Several minutes later we both had one that matched. She compared each to the one on the map. "They are identical in every way," Annie said.

"Do you remember where in the Valley of the Ancients these are located?" I asked.

"Not off the top of my head," she said, "but once we get there I should be able to easily. "

"Annie," I said, "I remember something else Mathew said. We were walking in the city and I asked him where the gold came from. He said 'we have a mine and it is full of gold. We don't mine it much anymore it is a treasure that we cherish for its looks and we use it to honor our gods by making their images out of gold.'"

Annie looked at me and said, "So the treasure is gold."

"It must," be I replied.

"Big Zach," she asked, "what did you bring with you when you left the Valley in the Mist?"

I thought for a minute and answered, "My pistols, my pouch, the clothes I had on and Big Jake."

"Where's the pouch Big Zach?" I handed it to her and she dumped it out. Nothing, but my reloads came out. She put her hand in and said nothing else. "Read it back to me again

Mathew's last words."

I picked up the paper and read it back. "Take this map. When we left our old homes we buried our treasure so no one would find it until we returned. We had no way of bringing it with us. He coughed and blood came from his mouth. I am dying, he said. Take the map and Zerena, leave this place. Save yourselves. He looked up at us and said follow Kokopelli patting the drawing on my shirt, he will lead you to the treasure of the ancients. He thrust the map into my hand and in a dying voice said your journey starts here and he died in Zerena's arms."

CHAPTER 11

"Where are the clothes you had on when you came back?"

"They're in a bag in your room."

Annie jumped up and brought out the bag dumping it on the floor. She picked up the shirt and said, "Look at this Big Zach," and turned the shirt around to face me. "Kokopelli just like the map." She turned it around and he was there again this time turned in the opposite direction.

She brought it over to the table and said, "Big Zach give me your knife." I handed it to her and she started to cut open the shirt at its seams. "Look Big Zach," she said very excited, "a map."

"Why that old coot, that's why he patted the Kokopelli on my shirt."

She cut the rest of the shirt open and there it was the map to the treasure of the ancients.

We studied it for quite a while neither of us speaking.

Finally Annie said, "See here, the same Kokopelli." She pointed to quite a few on the map. "Just like Mathew said, 'Kokopelli will lead you to the treasure'. See the Kokopelli's on the map lead south, see this pyramid here. It's Aztec and I may have been here depending on what city this is."

"I thought only the Egyptians had pyramids?" I asked.

"No Big Zach, many cultures had them. Look here the Kokopelli's lead to another pyramid and then to another only to return to the Valley of the Ancients. Some of this map may be a ruse to throw off anyone not an Anasazi. Or each place may give another clue to where the treasure is buried. They didn't want just anyone to find their treasure. If you didn't at least know a little bit about their culture you would never find the treasure. I hope we know enough, but we won't know until we get there."

"Annie," I said, "do you have a safe place we can put these until we leave?"

"I was just thinking the same thing."

She went over to the wall by the kitchen and pulled the rug over. She bent down and removed a board. A large metal box lay on the bottom. She put the maps in and replaced the floor and rug.

"They should be safe here," she said and yawned.

It was getting late, so Annie fixed us something to eat and we called it a night.

I got up early the next morning to sunshine and put some coffee on to boil. Big Jake wanted out so I opened the door and let him out to do his business.

Annie got up a few minutes later and I gave her a hug and a kiss.

"Morning," I said. "You sure are pretty in the morning."

She slapped me on the rump and went into the kitchen to pour us some coffee. Big Jake was at the door so I let him back in. He went into the kitchen and lay by the warm stove. Annie fixed breakfast and we got ready to go to Efren's.

When Annie was ready we left the house and walked up the street.

"I'll get us a cab when I see one," I said.

"No problem," answered Annie, "it's a beautiful morning for a walk."

Big Jake thought so too.

Ten minutes later we found a cabbie and he dropped us off at Efren's. "Hey Efren," I called, "you here?"

He answered, "Back here," and Big Jake beat us to him.

"Morning Efren," I said.

He said morning back and I saw he already had the horses saddled. "Thanks for saddling the horses," I said.

"No problem," he replied. "I knew you wanted to get an early start. I got everything on the horses but this." He held up the leather sack I had made to carry Big Jake on the horse.

"What is this contraption anyway?" he cackled.

"I had it made to carry Big Jake on the horse. It's too far for him to run along with the horses all the way, so he will be able ride when he gets tired. Look here," I said and put it on over the saddle bags tying it off. I put Big Jakes harness on and told him to "hup."

He jumped up and I put his feet into the sack and tied him down.

"Well I'll be," said Efren, "good idea you have there."

"We're off Efren, see you in four or five hours."

"Ok," he said.

I turned and Annie was already on Thunder. I pitched myself into the saddle, spurred Buck and chased Annie down the road and out of town.

CHAPTER 12

"You sure got you a mighty pretty horse there Miss Annie," I joked.

"Old Buck there ain't exactly an old plow horse either," she laughed.

"If I wasn't already spoke for I just might try to see what's in those britches," I quipped.

"Where is this Trollip?" she asked, "I'll shoot her in the ass. "

We both howled with laughter. "See that big tree way up ahead?" I said. "Let's see how these two can run."

"What's the bet?" Annie asked.

"Loser buys dinner."

"You're on," and Annie spurred Thunder into a run.

I was a little late, but Buck dug in and caught Thunder with a few yards to go and finished ahead of Annie.

"Wow," she said, "can this horse run. You may have beat me this time, but after I get used to Thunder we'll try again."

"Sure," I said, "I can always use a free meal." We both laughed and I pulled up. "Annie let's try out our guns and see if the horses are ok with the noise. That tree over there; put Thunder sideways to it and shoot at it."

Annie went over, pulled her pistol and fired into the tree. Thunder didn't move an inch.

"Now shoot over his head," I said. Annie moved Thunder into position and fired again.

She came back over to me and said, "Pretty calm, you try."

I walked Buck over and turned him sideways to the tree and drew my pistol and fired. Buck backed up a little, but seemed ok with the noise. I turned him toward the tree and fired again. He just stood there.

"Well we know we can shoot from horseback without landing in the dirt. Let's try another," I said, "those three trees along the road. Gallop Thunder by each and fire into them as you pass by."

"Ok," Annie said and spurred Thunder. She came to the first tree and fired, the next and fired and the last and fired.

"Go see how you did."

Annie rode back past each tree and said, "All hits."

"Good shooting," I replied. "My turn," I said and spurred Buck, drew and fired, again and again. I rode back past and said, "All hits. Let's take a break," I said and got off Buck.

I untied Big Jake and let him have a break too. He took off nose to the ground and we sat under a tree.

"Annie," I said. "I learned something from an old mountain man years ago that saved my life several times."

"Oh," said Annie, "and what is that?"

"He told me when you get done shooting reload your gun right then. If you put it off and forget you may need it when you least expect it and then you'll be dead."

We both reloaded our pistols and called over Big Jake and had him hup back on Buck. I put him into the sack and tied him down.

"Ok Annie," I said, "let's see what Thunder can do. Show me how he reins." She took Thunder a ways up the road and went through all his maneuvers.

"Can he back up?" I asked

She pulled back on the reins and he backed up. She came back to us and commented on how his previous owner must have spent a lot time training him.

"Yes," I said, "both these horses are very well trained. We'll need them where we're going. When we have some time there's more we can teach them. We'll do that on the trail. Let's head back," I said, and we turned the horses toward town.

We were just coming up on town when two riders came out from both sides of the road with their guns drawn.

"Hands up!" the man on our left said.

I raised mine, but Annie just sat there.

"Give us your gold," the other one said.

"Sorry boys," I said, "but I ain't got no gold."

"You think we're stupid mister?" the same one asked.

"Don't matter what I think," I said, "I still don't have any gold."

Just then Annie spoke. "Boys," she said, I got something better than gold batting her eyes. She moved her leg over the saddle showing some nice leg, both men fidgeted in their saddles.

"What would that be lady?"

"Lead," she said and drew and fired, they both flew out of their saddles and died in the road.

I looked at Annie her two smoking pistols and the dead men in the road.

"Let's get!" I said to Annie, "and remind me not to piss you off."

We made it to Efren's without any more trouble. I got down and let Big Jake off the horse.

"You two have a good time?" Efren asked.

"Yes Efren, we did," I replied. "Did you know Annie has a very bad temper?"

"No," he said, "and apparently you didn't either."

We all laughed and Efren said he'd tend to the horses. We said thanks and headed out to get my free dinner.

We had a nice meal at Ma's, and Big Jake had his usual steak medium rare. I grabbed a cabbie and twenty minutes later we arrived at Annie's.

We all went in and sat on the couch.

"Annie," I said, "you know anyone close by that has a corral we could use for one night?"

"Mr. Winston across the road has a barn and I think he is horse poor right now."

"Ok, I'll go talk to him and see if we can use it for one night."

I walked out and crossed the street; a man was standing in his yard.

"You be Mr. Winston?" I asked.

"Yes sonny what can I do for you?" he asked.

"Annie said you might have a barn we can keep our horses in for one night."

"Annie," he said. "Yep the barns over there, but I ain't got no hay or feed."

"That's ok," I said, "we can provide that. How much for the night we have four horses?"

"What say two dollars?" Mr. Winston said.

"Fine with me," and I paid him.

I walked back into the house and told Annie I paid him two dollars for the night. She said, "That old skin flint, I should have went over, I could have got it for a dollar."

"Or else," I commented, "you'd have shot him in the ass."

We both laughed. I looked over to the place we hid the maps and it looked the same as we left it.

CHAPTER 13

We were sitting on the couch and I asked Annie if she was still ok with the trip we were going to take.

"Yes Big Zach I am. I need to do this for two reasons. One, you asked me and the other is for my father. He would have jumped at a chance like this."

"Good Annie," I said and kissed her long and hard. She grabbed my hand and took me into the bedroom.

I rolled out of bed early the next morning and got dressed. I let Annie sleep while I made some coffee. I let Big Jake out and watched him while he relieved himself and called him back in. He ran into the bedroom and landed right on Annie's chest.

"Well good morning to you to Big Jake!" He licked her face and wagged his stump of a tail. "Where's that big galoot Big Zach at this morning? Probably gawking at the neighbor lady through her window."

"The big galoot is right here and the neighbor lady put on a nice show for me."

"Oh, better than this?" Annie said pulling the covers open.

"Nope," I said, "not that good." I jumped on the bed and had my way with Annie.

We finally got up and dressed. "We have a big day Annie," I said. "We need to provision and bring the horses over to Mr. Winston's."

"I'll be ready in a minute see if you can get a cabbie."

I found one right away and we headed to town to go shopping.

"You know Annie," I said, "its tradition to buy a new hat every time you go on a long trip."

"Oh," she said, "and I also heard its tradition not to let anyone see before they leave."

"To the haberdashery shop," I told the cabbie.

He dropped us off and we went inside.

"My, oh my Mister!" a skinny balding man said, "we don't let bears in our shop."

We laughed and I said, "How about dogs? Oh my sir no, no, no, not even dogs."

"Not even if that dog has gold to buy two new hats?" I said.

"Well, well, oh my," he stammered. "I guess it will be ok this once. What can I help you find."

Annie looked around and found the one she wanted. "Turn around Big Zach," and she handed it to the clerk. "I'll take this one, but wrap it up so he can't see it."

He complied and I told Annie to turn around. "This one will do just fine," I said, "and wrap it up the same."

He wrapped both hats and I paid him.

We walked out and went into another store to buy what we needed for the trip. We came out a few hours later and I hailed a cabbie. It took a few minutes to load up and we went back to Annie's. I told the cabbie to wait while we unloaded our goods and put them in the house. We came out a few minutes later and I told the cabbie to take us to Efren's.

When we arrived at Efren's he already had the horses saddled and the packhorses ready to go.

"Efren old friend," I said, "we'll both miss you!"

Annie gave him a kiss on his cheek. Efren stood there kind of teary eyed not saying anything, and we said our goodbyes.

We mounted up and left for Annie's. I looked over at Annie and she was praising her horse. She really loved that critter. I looked back at Big Jake and knew how she felt. We arrived and I put the horses in Mr. Winston's barn. I took the packs and went into the house. Annie was already packing so I just did the same. We had purchased some oilskin packets and I gave a few to Annie.

"Here Annie," I said, "help to keep our powder and caps dry."

Several hours later we were packed and ready to go.

"It's near March," I said to Annie, "by the time we get to Arizona Territory it will be spring."

"I am really excited," she said. "I won't sleep a wink."

"We'll lay down and try anyway," I said. "Big day tomorrow. I hope to be twenty five or thirty miles from St. Louis by tomorrow night."

We ate our last meal and went to bed. Big Jake knew we were leaving and spent the night on the bed. He didn't want to be left out.

I didn't sleep much and neither did Annie. We finally got up, dressed and I went to get the horses. When I returned Annie had her new hat on.

"Well what do you think?" she asked.

"I think you look just fine. The hat suits you."

I reached over the couch, grabbed mine and put it on. "Well Annie?" I said.

She replied that she would have to think about it. I swatted her on the rump and we saddled up and loaded the packs on the packhorses. I put Big Jake's harness on and had him hup up on Buck. I tied him down and said, "You ready Annie?"

"Yes Big Zach, let's go."

So we took to the trail and it was just getting light when I noticed Annie turn around and take a last look at her home. She turned back around and smiled at me. "I love you Big Zach."

"I love you too Annie," I said and we left St. Louis behind.

Several hours later we boarded a ferry to take us over to the other side of the Mississippi. I heard one of the ferrymen say, "Nice set," and the other said, "Yah nice horses."

I smiled and the other said, "I wasn't talking about the horses."

I looked at him and smiled broader.

We came to a stop on the other side, mounted up and went on our way.

"Annie," I said, "we need to talk about the dangers out here. There are some bad men and of course Indians. These horses are worth a lot of money and of course you being a woman," I said.

She just looked at me and said, "Glad you noticed!" and we both laughed.

"One thing we need to pay attention to is our back trail. Keep your head on a swivel out here; danger can come from any direction. I probably don't need to say this to you, but if you need to shoot, shoot to kill not in the ass."

We both had a good laugh.

Big Jake had been enjoying the trip so far, but it was time to let him trail. I stopped and untied him. "Big Jake," I said, "trail," and he took off with his nose to the ground. Sometimes he would get pretty far away and then wait for us to catch up. It was a nice day and we were making good time.

CHAPTER 14

Long about sundown we stopped and camped. I found a spot off the trail that we could defend and not be seen by others. I hobbled the horses and let them graze.

Annie spoke up and said, "Big Zach what would you like for dinner, bacon with your beans or beans with your bacon?"

"I like 'em both ways" I said smiling.

After we had eaten and cleaned up. We were sitting by the fire and I said, "Here are a few more things to think about as we get further from civilization. If you look directly into the fire it will ruin your night vision for quite a while, so look around the fire not at it. This will be the last time we eat where we camp. Next time we'll stop, eat and then move several miles away to camp."

"Can we have coffee?" she asked.

"Not at night, but we can make some in the morning. When we cook the evening meal we'll make enough for breakfast and eat it on the trail. When we get to the hill country we'll stay off the ridges, a man on horse can be seen from a long way off."

"You need to know a few things about Big Jake." His ears pricked up. "See how he's lying. Towards the road," I said.

"Yes," she replied.

"He always sleeps so he can warn us if anyone comes our way. He sleeps real light and he'll give us plenty of notice. You already knows he hates Indians. If there is an Indian within five miles he can smell them. He lets out a low growl and you know its Indians."

I went through his hand signals with Annie and she was amazed how smart he was. "He's double tuff and mean as a snake when he has to be, but we need to keep him safe from himself. He'll tackle a grizzly bear, but we don't want to get him hurt or killed."

"Yes Big Zach, I understand," Annie said.

"One more thing and we'll get some sleep. Always keep a pistol within easy reach when you sleep, and sleep light. You may have to wake up fast and defend yourself. We sleep with our clothes on and our boots off."

I reached over and gave Annie a kiss goodnight.

We woke early and I had coffee on the boil.

"I need to relieve myself Annie," said to me.

"Take the shovel with you and bury anything you do. Harder for anyone to find where we been. Take Big Jake with you."

"Come on Big Jake," she said, "you can guard me while I pee."

I shook my head and got breakfast ready. We left shortly after and headed west toward the Valley of the Ancients.

The next five days saw us near a small settlement. I stopped and got down. I put Big Jake's harness on and had him hup onto Buck. I tied him down and looked at Annie. Annie turned to look at our back trail.

"Dust back there Big Zach. Hand me the telescope," she said.

I gave it to her and a minute later she said, "Two riders coming fast and there right on our trail."

She handed me the telescope and I took a look. "May be just a coincidence, but something don't feel right." I looked around and found us a place to put the horses out of sight.

"How far Annie?" I asked.

"Maybe ten minutes away."

"Ok, get up there behind those rocks and don't show yourself until you have to. I'll get over here and if there's trouble we'll have them in a cross fire. Get ready," and we took our positions.

The men following us galloped to a stop right in front of us.

"Where'd they go Zeke?" asked the skinny one.

"I don't know, but I want that girl."

I had heard enough and stood up with both pistols in my hands. "We didn't go anywhere boys were right here," I said.

"Damn," said the big one. "Hey you mister," he said, "all we want is the girl and you can be on your way."

"What girl?" I said.

"We know you was the one with the girl and we mean to have her." "Where'd you see me and the girl at?" I asked.

"Don't never mind, you gonna give to her to us or not?"

"What do you think Annie?" I yelled.

Annie stood up both pistols in her hand. "I think I'd rather sit on a cactus than let you get within ten feet of me you low down dirty scum suckers." Just then I saw him reach for his gun and I shot him out of the saddle. Annie let loose and the skinny fella went off his horse dead. I climbed back down and turned the big fella over.

"You know him Annie?"

"No Big Zach and him neither," she said pointing to the skinny one. "They sure wanted you," I said.

"They got what they deserved and the devil has them now," she replied.

"Well let's round up their horses and take 'em in to that settlement up ahead, maybe there's law there."

An hour later we had them loaded and went on in to town. I stopped by an old man sitting on a porch and asked if there was any law in town. "Sorta," he said, "the blacksmith sometimes be's the sheriff."

We went on down to the blacksmith's shop and stopped. He was pounding on a horse shoe.

"Hey there," I shouted, "you be the sheriff here about?"

"I guess so what can I do for you?"

"I got these two varmints here that need burying."

"So what do you want me to do with them?"

"Bury them," I said.

He walked over and lifted the big ones head and said, "Well it'll be Zeke Cromwell and I'll bet the others his pard Skinny Jones." He walked over and lifted the other fellas head. "Yep that's him. You sure saved the people in these parts some heartache. These two been making trouble around here for months."

"You going to bury them?" I asked.

"You shot them you bury them," he said.

"Tell you what," I said, "you can keep their horses, their guns and any money you find on them."

He looked at me and Annie and said, "Ok mister I'll do it."

I handed him the reins and we left town. I wanted to get us as far away as I could from that place.

CHAPTER 15

We rode west and I said to Annie, "Where do you think them boys saw us?"

"I've been thinking on that, and the only place I can come up with is the ferry, but that was five days ago." Replied Annie

"Sit on a cactus then let you get within ten feet of me you low down dirty scum suckers," I laughed.

"Well the skinny one was sorta cute," she replied.

We laughed for hours about that. We stopped for a rest and I let Big Jake down. He needed to get the kinks out and trail for a while.

Five more days and we didn't' see a soul. We came over a small ridge and down at the bottom was a large cabin. I stopped and we both got down.

"What you make of it Big Zach?" Annie asked.

"Not sure, but we better watch for a while and see if anyone comes out."

Just then Big Jake growled low. "Indians!" I said, "get down."

We both hunkered down and looked around. I couldn't see anyone moving about. Then Big Jake started to get excited. I told him to quit and looked down the way he was looking. Then I saw them; six of them sneaking up on the cabin. Just then we heard a shot and one of the Indians went down.

"The cabin is defending itself," I said.

The Indians crept closer and we heard another shot. The Indian closet to the cabin went down. I got up and got my rifle.

"We need to help them," said Annie.

"I know," I replied. "They don't know we're here so maybe we can surprise them. I'll take the ones on the right and you take out the two on the left. We'll start the ball after I use the rifle."

I aimed and fired hitting one of the Indians on the right. Annie let loose and killed both the ones on the left. Another shot from the cabin killed the last one.

"I'll stand guard you reload." I said

Annie quickly reloaded and she watched while I did the same.

"Hey the cabin," I shouted.

"Who you be out there?" a voice from the cabin said.

"Friends," I replied.

"Come on in friends and welcome."

We both looked around and Big Jake didn't alert, so we mounted up and slowly made our way to the cabin. I dismounted and just then the door opened. An old short balding man and his wife came out the door.

"Hi," I said, "names Zach Taylor and this is Annie."

"Look Martha a gal. My name is Otto and this is my wife Martha. Please come in."

We went in and the place was very large. "It's a store," said Annie.

"Yes," said Otto, "an oasis in the desert."

There was about anything you could want there.

"Thank you so much for helping us with those Indians," said Otto. "They have been trying to kill us for several months. Please, please," Otto said, "my manners please sit."

We took chairs and Big Jake sat looking at a rather large piece of jerky hanging from the top of the counter.

"My word," said Otto.

"I thought he was a bear at first, but what a beautiful dog you have," Martha said. "Can I pet him?"

"Sure," I said, "Big Jake touch," and he went over to her.

She scratched and petted him. "He is so soft," Martha said. "What breed is he?"

I was about to speak when Annie said proudly, "He is a Bouvier des Flandres and he comes from Belgium."

"What an odd dog to be in this country. Where you folks going?" Otto asked.

Annie was about to speak, but I said, "Colorado. We have folks up that a way we haven't seen for quite some time. Say Otto," I asked, "you wouldn't happen to have a nice cold beer would you?"

"Ah," he said, "my manners again. Yes we do and would the young lady want something too?"

Annie spoke up and said, "A glass of cold water would be nice."

"Martha can you get these young people a drink."

"Yes father," she said and left.

"Where are we anyway Otto?" Annie asked.

"Why you don't know?" he said.

"No we were hoping you could tell us."

Martha came in and handed us both a drink. "Texas," Martha said proudly.

"We have come a long way Big Zach," Annie said.

"Where did you come from?" Martha asked.

"St. Louis," Annie responded.

"My you have come a long way."

"Say Otto," I said, "you sell any of this?" I asked waving my hand.

"Yes anything you like."

I looked at Annie and she said, "Beans, a sack of flour salt, sugar, coffee. And that big hunk of that jerky hanging there."

Martha pulled a hunk from the jerky and threw it towards Big Jake. He caught it and had it down before you could wink.

"What a smart dog," she said.

"You don't know the half it," Annie said. "He's the one that saved your lives. If he hadn't alerted us to those Indians well... He's my hero," said Annie.

Big Jake put his front feet on her lap and licked her face.

"Do you have water Otto?" I asked.

"Yes cold and sweet and all you want."

"Can I get some for the horses?"

"Sure come with me."

We went outside and he uncovered a well. I filled several buckets and gave the horses a big drink.

"Get your canteens and I'll help fill them."

"Otto," I said, "can we also get that canvas water bag you have?"

"Sure," he said and went inside to fetch it.

When I went back in I saw Big Jake had a big bowl of water he was drinking.

"How much we owe you Otto?" I said.

"Martha will get the total for you," he said.

"Can I ask where the nearest large settlement is from here?"

"Well let's see, Santa Fe and Albuquerque are both on your way. Albuquerque is bigger, but they are both nice towns."

"How far?" Annie asked.

"About two weeks ride, maybe more," Otto answered. "Just head west and you run right into Albuquerque. Santa Fe is a little farther north." We paid our bill and loaded up the supplies.

"Thanks for everything," I said.

Otto and Martha waved till we were out of sight.

CHAPTER 16

We made our way west and just as Otto had said we made Albuquerque twelve days later. We slowly made our way down Main Street.

"I love this southwestern atmosphere and the Mexicans are very nice people," Annie said.

I spotted a livery and we road over to it. A small Mexican man met us at the door. "Hola," he said, "welcome to Albuquerque Senor and Senorita. My name is Juan."

"Thank you Juan can we board our horses here?" I asked.

"Yes Senor it is ten cents a day with hay, grain is ten cents extra. I will also throw in a rub down for the horses also. How long will you be staying?" he asked.

I looked at Annie and said, "Several days amigo."

Annie cracked a big smile. "The pack horses you can feed and rub down, but these two are a might unfriendly to strangers so we can rub them down and you can feed them."

"Ok Senor come this way."

He led us to some stalls in the back and we unsaddled the horses.

"Juan, do you know anywhere we could put our gear so it's safe?" I asked.

"Yes Senor we have a locked room. No charge," he said smiling.

We put up our gear and finished rubbing down the horses. I grabbed my rifle and some clothes. Annie grabbed a big bag she had brought and we went outside.

"Juan," I called.

"Yes Senor."

"What's the best Hotel in town?"

"The Desert Inn Senor. It even has baths indoors. Look at the end of the street it is there," he said.

We grabbed our gear and walked down the street. When we got to the hotel we walked in and was met by a nice Mexican gentleman. "Welcome to the Desert Inn Senor and Senorita," he said. "My name is Manuel. What can I do for you?"

"We need a room and two hot baths."

"How long will you be staying with us?' he asked.

"Three, maybe four days," I said.

"Very good will you sign in please."

I signed in as Mr. and Mrs. Taylor. "I see you have a perro with you."

"A what?" I asked.

"Big Jake," Annie said.

"Oh yes," I said.

"He is also welcome. Your room is on first floor in the back. The sun does not shine so much there."

I paid Manuel and he gave us the key. "Room 101," he said.

Annie glanced at the hotel register and said, "Has a nice ring to it and smiled.

"Senor I almost forgot. I will have your baths ready in half an hour."

We went to our room and the first thing Annie did was flop down on the bed. "A bed, a real bed for three nights. You trying to spoil me Big Zach."

"Yes, young lady I am."

I joined her on the bed and we kissed. There was a knock on the door and I got up to answer it. "Senor and Senorita your baths are ready please follow me."

We grabbed our gear and followed the young man to a door down the hall. Annie went in and I stopped to give the young man a nickel. "Gracias," he said and ran away. I locked the door and stripped throwing my clothes in a pile. Annie was a bit slower and I watched her undress.

"See anything you like mister?" she asked.

"No, no," I said, "just looking at the nice drapes."

She threw water in my face and I got into her tub. The water was hot and soothing. We stayed in them for over an hour. When I was done I put Big Jake in and scrubbed him up and down. He loves the water and the bath made him feel as good as we did.

We went back to our room and Annie said "It's early, let's get dressed and go see the sights."

"Ok," I said, "let's do just that."

When we went by the front desk I asked if we could get our clothes washed and dried.

"Si Senor," he said.

"There in a pile in our room."

"I will take care of it for you," he said and we walked outside.

It was a beautiful day, but not hot. Big Jake dried off in no time and we went to see the sights. There were street merchants everywhere selling all kinds of things. We passed a table and something caught my eye. It was a silver Kokopelli with a silver chain. What was interesting was it was just like the one on the map. Was this just a coincidence or an omen?

"How much for this?" I asked.

"Fifty cents American," the lady said.

I paid her and put the charm in my pocket. "May I ask who made the charm?"

"Yes, he is my grandfather."

"Would I be able to speak to him?"

"Si senor, but he will not be here until tomorrow. Come back then and you can speak to him."

I thanked her and caught up with Annie. "See anything you like?" I asked.

"Yes I like it all," Annie replied, "but look at this. Isn't it the most beautiful dress you have ever seen?"

"Yes," I said, "buy it."

"You sure Big Zach?"

"Why not a beautiful dress for a beautiful lady." She paid the lady and she handed her the bag.

We walked most of the day and I said, "I hear they have some real good food here."

"Yes," Annie said excitedly, "very good food. Let's find us a restaurant."

Most every restaurant we passed had outside seating so it was no problem sitting with Big Jake. The waiter came to us and said, "Hola my name is Jose and I will be your waiter. Can I get you anything to drink?" "Yes," I said. "Annie what's your pleasure?"

"Something cold and refreshing," she said.

"And you senor?"

"A nice cold beer," I said.

"Very well I will be right back."

He returned in minutes and set the drinks down. I took a sip and downed the whole glass. Annie looked at me and laughed. "You must have been thirsty Big Zach!"

"Yes, and that was marvelous."

"Would you like another?" he said.

"Yes," I said, "but with dinner."

"What may I get for you?" he asked.

I looked at Annie and she said, "Two beef enchiladas and some tortilla chips and salsa, and a large steak cooked medium rare."

He nodded and left.

CHAPTER 17

I pulled out the charm I had bought and held it in my closed hand.

"What do have there?" she asked.

"A present for a beautiful young lady."

"What do I have to do for it?" she asked.

"Well how about letting me watch you put on that beautiful dress."

"Deal now give me the present." Said Annie.

I opened my hand and she picked up the charm. "It is beautiful," she said, "and solid silver." Annie put it on and looked at the Kokopelli. She looked up and then back down at the charm. "Big Zach did you notice anything funny about this?" she said.

"Yes, it looks just like the Kokopelli on the map."

"Coincidence or…?"

"I don't know, but I asked the lady who sold it to me who made it. She said her grandfather did. I asked her if we could talk to him, but he won't be back until tomorrow."

"I wonder where he got this image from."

"Hopefully we'll know tomorrow."

The food arrived and we had a very nice meal. Big Jake as always thought his steak was just fine. I asked the waiter how long they would be open, and he said it was fiesta all week and that they were open until eleven or twelve each night.

We left and I said to Annie, "I think we should go see the horses. Make sure everything is ok."

"Ok," she said, and we went down to the livery.

We checked the horses and everything was fine. I asked Juan if he could open the door so we could get something from our packs.

He said, "sure" and opened the door. I rummaged through and found the maps. "Maybe we should keep these close," I said.

Annie nodded and we left for the hotel.

Once in our room we laid on the bed and closed our eyes for a few minutes and woke up with the sun going down.

"How long have we been asleep?" Annie asked?

"I'm not sure, but I'd say four or five hours. Let's get cleaned up and you put that pretty dress on and go to the fiesta."

Annie squeaked, "Can we Big Zach?"

"Sure why not? I think I'll leave Big Jake here though. I can hear fireworks and fire crackers going off everywhere."

There was knock on the door and I opened it. "Senor your clothes are cleaned," and he handed them to me.

"What do I owe you?" I said

"Nothing today, but when you leave." I handed him a nickel and closed the door.

"I could get use to this," I said.

"I know, aren't' the Mexican people just wonderful."

Annie changed into her new dress and we went out for a night on the town. We came back late and Big Jake was really glad to see us. I took him out to relieve himself and we got ready for bed.

The next morning the sun was shining and it looked like a beautiful day. "Get dressed Annie and let's go for a walk and have breakfast."

"Be with you in a minute," she said.

We walked down toward where the table was where I had purchased the Kokopelli charm but no one was there yet. So we walked to the end of town and found a nice outside café and had breakfast. Big Jake looked hungry so I ordered him another steak. I paid for our meal and we left walking back to the hotel.

The lady that sold me the Kokopelli was just setting up and we walked over to her.

"Remember me?" I said. "I was wanting to talk to your grandfather."

"Yes," she said, "he is here I will get him."

A very old man walked out and I greeted him holding out my hand. He looked more Indian than Mexican, but Big Jake didn't alert.

"Hola," I said, and asked him if he spoke English.

"Yes," he said, "I do speak English."

Annie showed him the necklace and he smiled.

"I bought this from your granddaughter yesterday."

"Yes," he said smiling.

"The Kokopelli you designed here, where did you get the picture to make it?" I asked.

He pointed to the north and said, "Many miles to the north. I use to live there many years ago."

I asked him how old he was, and he said he was one hundred and ten. Both Annie and I were shocked.

I asked him if he was an Indian and he said, "Yes I am a descendent of the Ancient Ones. We lived in the homes on the cliffs when I was young, but no more. We are all, but gone. I am the only one left."

"Could you draw us a map of where you lived?" I asked. "I will pay you."

He nodded and went to get some paper. Annie and I watched as he drew a map to the city he lived in years ago.

"There are mountains on each side and a valley in the middle." He scratched out the trail to follow to the valley and put an 'x' close to the trail over half way to the valley. "It is a long way," he said, "maybe..." he searched for an answer and asked his granddaughter.

"He says two weeks to walk."

"Do you know the name of the valley you lived in?" I asked.

He spoke through his granddaughter again. "He says the Valley of the Ancients."

"What is this?" I asked pointing to the 'x' on the map.

"It is a small town."

"What is there?" I asked again.

His granddaughter interrupted. "The town," she said. "is called Anasazi and it has a small cantina and a store. A hardware store and food."

I asked the old man if he would guide us to the valley.

"No, no," he said.

"I will pay you," I said.

"No, no," he said again, "defender," and walked away.

I thanked his granddaughter and gave her two dollars. "See he gets this will you?" I asked.

"Yes Senor, I will give to him."

We left and went back to the hotel. "Well what do you make of that?" Annie said, "the last of the Anasazi?"

We walked slowly back to the hotel. "Big Zach, you see anything odd in the old man when you asked if he'd guide us?"

"Yes," I said, "he looked worried."

"I wonder why?" asked Annie.

"I think I know Annie. Remember the story of the Valley in the Mist. Who was Tomo?"

"He was a defender!" exclaimed Annie.

"And the old man said 'No, no defender.'"

"What does it mean Big Zach?"

"It means we may have company when we get to the Valley of the Ancients."

We continued our walk back to the hotel when Big Jake alerted with his low growl. "Indians," Annie said.

I looked in the direction Big Jake was looking and it was an alley. I told him to quit and we continued toward the hotel. When we got next to the alley Big Jake alerted and this time he was very adamant. I told Big Jake to quit, stopped and turned to Annie. "Smile," I said, and she looked at me smiling.

"What do you see in the alley?' I asked? "Keep smiling and talk to me," I said.

"Well there is a man standing in the shadows looking at us."

I said, "Follow me," and we kept on walking to the next block. I grabbed Annie and we hid around the corner. I pulled my pistol and said, "Wait here. I'm going to see what's going on. If I flush him out tell Big Jake to hold and he will not let the man leave without a few bites."

Annie pulled her pistol.

"Give me two minutes and go back around the corner."

I ran to the other corner of the building then to the corner of the alley. I carefully looked around the corner and the man was still there. He was looking at the street so I silently crept up on him. Walking quietly was something you learned living in the mountains. I got right up to him and stuck the pistol on the back of neck. He froze and I cocked the pistol. I turned him around and put him against the wall. Stepping into the street I motioned Annie to come over. I grabbed the man and took him to the end of the alley and pushed him down. Big Jake came running up and stuck his snarling face against the man's face. He was shaking badly. I told Big Jake to quit and he backed up a foot ready to pounce if the man moved. I looked at him and he was an Indian, but what tribe I didn't know.

"You speak English?" I asked.

He just sat there shaking. I pulled him up and searched him for weapons. I found a knife and threw it away.

"Annie let's see if there is some law in this town."

We both put our pistols away and walked to the front of the street. "Annie," I said, "ask that vendor if there is a sheriff or some kind of law here."

She had a short conversation with the lady and motioned me to follow her. She said "Next corner turn right and his office is there."

We made our way to the sheriff's office and I pushed the Indian threw the door.

CHAPTER 18

"What's this the man at the desk?" said standing up.

"Hi," I said. "This man has been following us. I tried to talk to him, but he won't answer me."

"Well mister you know why he can't answer?"

"No," I said.

"Because he don't speak English. He's a harmless old Navajo, this town's beggar and all around pain in my ass. His name is Nakai."

The sheriff spoke to him in a language I had never heard. The Indian responded.

"I asked him why he was following you," the sheriff said, "and he says a white man paid him to follow you and tell him where you go."

"Ask him where this white man is right now," I said.

The sheriff translated and the Indian responded once again. "He says he's sitting in the cantina at the end of the street."

"Which cantina?" I asked.

The sheriff asked him and he pointed. "He says the one with the red flowers. That would be Rosie's," the sheriff said.

"Can you ask him what the man looks like and what he is wearing."

"He says a white suit and hat. He is a very big man." He pointed to me, "Just as big as you or bigger."

"Thanks sheriff," I said, and we went out the door with the sheriff asking what was going on.

"I think this cantina is right across the street from the hotel," Annie said.

"Ok, let's walk on down and see if we can find this mysterious rather large white man in the white suit."

We walked on down the street and as we got closer we both saw the man the Indian had described.

"Big Zach," Annie said, "I know that man."

I looked at her and we kept walking. When we were abreast of him we walked over and I told Big Jake to watch. He jumped over the railing and put his two inch fangs on the man's face.

"You mister!" I said, "why are you having us followed?" I asked.

"Call your dog off mister," he said, "or else."

"Or else what?' I replied.

"Or I'll kill him."

His hand went to his gun and Annie pulled hers and pointed it at his head, "You do Martin and you'll be dead one second later." His hand left his pistol and I told Big Jake to quit. He came back over to me and sat.

"Well, Annie Stillwell," he said.

"Yes Martin it's me."

Martin got himself back under control and wiped his face. "It's been a long time Annie."

"Five years," she said, "and I was hoping you were dead."

"No Annie I'm not dead yet," he said smiling.

"The day ain't over yet Martin," she said pointing the gun at his head. "Now, now Annie no need for that."

"Then why are you having us followed?" she said. "And it had better be good." Annie was really pissed off at this guy and she meant what she said.

"I wasn't having you followed per say. I was just curious why you were back in the southwest again after your father's accident."

75

"Accident my ass," she said, "he was murdered and I think you know who did it."

"I had nothing to do with your father's demise," he said.

"You're a liar, a thief and a murderer. If I see you anywhere around us again I'm not going to say a word. I'm just going to pull this pistol and empty it in your skunk ridden hide. You hear me Martin?"

"Yes Annie I hear you, now put down the gun and let me buy you both a cool drink."

"Remember what I said Martin," and she grabbed me and called Big Jake.

We went back to the Hotel and I stopped at the door. "Annie," I asked, "what in the hell was that all about?"

She was still fuming and said, "Not here Big Zach, in our room."

We walked to our room and Big Jake alerted in his 'Indians are here' growl. I pushed Annie next to the wall. I told Big Jake to quit and motioned Annie to be quiet. I got next to our room door and pulled my pistol. Annie had her pistol out and I motioned to her holding up my fingers. One, two, three and I crashed through the door. A very large Indian was bent over the bed looking at our maps. He saw us and leaped for the window. Big Jake was right after him and took a big chunk out of his ass. The Indian finally made it through the window and I called off Big Jake. I went to the window and looked out. The Indian was nowhere to be seen.

"This have anything to do with your friend out there Annie?" I asked. "Yes," she said, "this smells just like that son of a bitch."

"Looks like he didn't take anything, the maps are still here, but I think he got a good look at them," I said.

Annie sat on the bed and put her hands on her face and cried. I sat next to her and wrapped my arm around her. She bent over and cried on my shoulder. "Oh Big Zach," she said, "I thought I'd never see that son of a bitch again."

"You think he had your father murdered?"

"Yes Big Zach I do." She dried her eyes and told me the story.

"Five years ago my father and Martin were commissioned by the university to find any clues as to what happened to the Anasazi. Remember when I told you we didn't find any gold in the Valley of the Ancients? Well that was only a half truth. We didn't find any trace except a rather large statue of their Sun God. It weighed over twenty pounds and was solid gold. Martin tried to get my father to steal it and they would split the money. My father was an honest decent man. He saw the statue as a link to the Anasazi. Something to be studied and put in a museum. Martin stormed away and we didn't see him again. My father kept up the search for artifacts and two days later I found him dead with Indian arrows sticking out of him. The gold statue was gone and so were Martin's things. I buried my father in the valley and went home. A year later I heard some professors talking about Martin being very well off, and they thought he must have had some kind of a windfall of money. I knew where he got the money. He sold the statue to highest bidder and made a lot of money, probably ten times what the gold was worth. Now he plunders, steals and murder's to get what he wants and he wants anything related to Native American Indians. He sells the artifacts to Europeans. They are fascinated with the North American Indian and will pay almost anything to get the artifacts. Now his man has seen the map and knows we are after something. He doesn't know its gold, but Big Zach we are in real danger. He will stop at nothing now that he knows we're looking for something in the Valley of the Ancients and we have a map."

CHAPTER 19

"Don't let anyone in except us."

"Where are you going?" Annie asked.

"To find me an Indian. Maybe I can catch him before he tells Martin what he's seen. Shoot to kill Annie," I said, and jumped out the same window the Indian made his escape from.

I told Big Jake to find and he turned sniffing the ground. He looked up and took off running down the alley. I followed him to the next street and he lost the scent. He looked up at me and I told him to find again. He scented all around and as I watched him his head turned and he took off up another alley. He had him now. Big Jake followed the scent two more streets down and went to a door. He stood their looking at me. I signed him to stay, pulled both my Colts and put my ear to the door.

"Well it took you long enough," I heard Martin say. "What happened to you?" Martin asked the Indian.

"Man's dog hurt me," and he showed Martin where Big Jake took a chunk out him.

"I'm going to kill that dog," Martin said. "What did you find?"

"Me find plenty, "the Indian said, and I broke the door down.

"Howdy Martin," I said, pointing one Colt at him and the other at the Indian. Big Jake came in right after me and snarled at the Indian.

"What right you got busting in here like this?" Martin asked.

"Same right you have getting this Indian to break into our hotel room." The Indian moved for his knife and Big

Jake had him by the throat before he even touched it. He tore out his throat and moved over to Martin blood dripping from his face. He inched toward Martin and I said, "Don't move a muscle or your dead."

Martin looked at Big Jake his eyes glued to the dog. I told Big Jake to quit and he came around me and sat.

"You ain't shit without that dog," he said.

"You think these Colts ain't shit either?" I said.

"And the guns," he added.

"So you think you're a tuff guy Martin, are you let's see." I holstered both Colts.

"What about the dog?" he said.

"Oh he won't bother you none." I told Big Jake to stay.

Martin jumped up and caught me in a bear hug. He had his fists against my lower back and it hurt like hell. He put more pressure on and I saw stars. I grabbed both his ears and gave him a head but on his nose. Blood went everywhere and he let go. I bent over to catch my breath and then hit him with a right uppercut that took him off his feet. He got up and came at me swinging both arms. I blocked his punches and grabbed him behind his head. I pulled his head down as hard as I could and lifted a knee into his face. I heard something crack and teeth went all over the place. I let him go and he fell down. I reached down and picked him up, and looked him in the eyes.

"If I ever see you again I'll hang you up by your feet and skin you alive. It may take a week, but I'll get every piece of skin off you and then feed you to the crows."

"Who are you?' he said through battered lips.

"Ask your Indian friends, they call me Obede Ittawa."

I threw him down and called Big Jake.

Martin got up and spat blood and teeth into his hands. "I'm going to kill that son of a bitch and his dog then have my way with Annie before I kill her too."

We rushed back to the hotel and I knocked on the window. Annie came over and opened it for us. We both scampered back in and sat down. "Big Zach you're hurt, and Big Jake he's all bloody."

"It's not ours," I said.

"What happened?" she said cleaning off my face.

"We found the Indian with Martin. I burst into his room just before the Indian told him about the map."

"So Martin doesn't know we have it?"

"The Indian made a move for his knife and Big Jake well..."

"Big Jake tore out his throat," said Annie.

"Yes," I said.

"What about Martin?" she asked.

"He thought he was a tuff man and I showed him the errors of his ways."

"Did you kill him?" Annie asked.

"No Annie I didn't, but I wanted to real bad. Martin won't be able to do much for at least a week other than eat threw a straw, I broke his jaw and he's missing a few teeth."

"We need to leave big Zach," Annie said.

"Yes I think we better. Tomorrow morning early. Let's get me and Big Jake cleaned up and go provision. I'll pay our bill on the way out and we can leave when we want to."

CHAPTER 20

On our way out to get supplies I told the hotel clerk to get our bill ready as we were leaving early the next morning. We bought what we needed and packed it away. Then we went back to the hotel and our bill was ready. I told Juan again we would be leaving early the next morning and we got something to eat at the cantina across from the hotel. After our meal we went back to the hotel and went to our room.

"Let's get packed up," I said to Annie.

"I thought we were going first thing in the morning?' Annie asked.

"I just told that to everyone. Martin probably has spies everywhere. He's already been told were leaving in the morning. So we don't get ambushed by his thugs we're leaving as soon as it gets dark."

The sun went down and we put all our gear out the window. I helped Annie out and Big Jake followed. We walked in the shadows and took the back way to the livery. I met Juan and told him we were leaving right now. I asked him to keep it to himself and paid him five dollars.

"Si senor," he said, "I will not tell a soul and he crossed his heart."

We were saddled and ready in no time and took off out the back door. I waved to Juan and we left for the Valley of the Ancients.

We spent the whole night and all the next day traveling. The trail took us way up into the mountains. When we came to good spot to stop for the night I got down and looked for any sign. Big Jake did the same only with his nose.

"Annie let's move the horses behind those rocks and make camp. We'll have a cold camp tonight and make breakfast in the morning. We can see our back trail for miles up here. If anyone follows we can see them."

Just before dark Annie went up on a rock and telescoped our back trail. "See anything?' I asked.

"No Big Zach, no one is there."

"Good let's settle in and get some sleep."

We sat around eating jerky and drinking water.

"Big Zach," Annie said. "You know Martin will follow us, or at least he will go to the Valley of the Ancients to see what were up to."

"Or send his Indian friends to do it," I said.

I told Annie to get some sleep and I would stand the first watch. Big Jake curled up next to her and they both slept. I was pretty tired, but this wasn't the place to let our guard down. We had Martin, the Indians and maybe the defenders to worry about. I found a good spot to watch the trail both ways and hunkered down. It was getting towards morning when Big Jake came up to me.

"Hi boy," I said. "You get enough sleep?" I asked scratching his ear.

He lay beside me and then Annie came over. "You were supposed to wake me," Annie said.

"I was just coming to get you," I lied.

"Sure you were," she said. "Get over there and get some sleep. Me and Big Jake can take it from here."

"Ok," I said and got up. "Wake me at first light we need to move on."

"Ok Big Zach, get some sleep."

I lay down on my blanket and was asleep seconds later.

Martin woke the next morning, he felt like a herd of buffalos had run him over. He got up anyway. He wanted to get to the Indian village before noon. He dressed and went over to put some water on his face. He looked in the mirror and said, "I'm going to kill that son of a bitch even if it kills me."

Most of his front teeth were gone and his face was black and blue. He saddled up and started up the mountain to the Indian village. He needed help and they knew the territory. He rode in about noon and went looking for the chief's daughter. She spoke English learning it from the mission school that was once there.

"Sitsi," he called, and she came out from a teepee nearby.

"Martin!" she said, "what is wrong, you look hurt?"

"Yes Sitsi I am. Had a little trouble last night in town."

"Where is Bidzial?" Sitsi asked.

"Well that's part of my trouble. Bidzial was killed by a fellow last night. Can I speak with your father?"

"I will see," and Sitsi left him standing by his horse.

She came out of a teepee and waved Martin over. "He will see you Martin."

Martin went in and the chief looked at him and said in Navajo, "What has happened?"

Sitsi translated and told the old chief what Martin had said. The chief spoke and Sitsi said, "He is very upset Martin. Bidzial was a strong warrior. He asked who killed him."

"Tell him a big white man. Said you know him. Said his name was Obede Ittawa."

The chief sat down and looked at the wall of the teepee. "You know him Chief?" Martin asked.

The chief began to talk. He spoke for several minutes and looked at Martin and kept speaking.

"Well Sitsi what did he say?"

"He says our brothers the Blackfoot to the far north know of him. He is the one they call death with a dog. He has killed many braves and his dog many more. They have sent hundreds of braves to kill him, but they never returned. He is bad medicine and he wants nothing to do with him. He says go and never return."

Martin left the teepee and was about to climb on his horse when a very large brave came to him. He spoke in guttural tones and Martin called Sitsi over.

"What's he saying to me?"

She listened and spoke. "His name is Nastas he is brother to Bidzial. He says who killed his brother?"

Sitsi told him and he got very upset.

"He says he is not afraid of Obede Ittawa. He says tell him where he is and he will kill him."

"Tell him it may take more than one brave to kill him." Martin said.

Sitsi explained. "He says he needs no one else to kill the one they call death with the dog. He wants to know where he can find him," Sitsi said.

"Tell him the Valley of the Ancients."

"I will go there," he said, "and take the scalp of the one they call Obede Ittawa and the hide of his dog."

Martin headed back to town. He wasn't sure one brave could get the job done so he needed some men of his own. Men that would kill their own mother for money and he knew just where to find them.

CHAPTER 21

Annie woke me a few hours later to the smell of coffee and bacon.

"That coffee sure smells good," I said. "I feel a lot better now." I went behind a rock and relieved myself.

Annie handed me a cup of coffee and a plate of pancakes and bacon. "Where's yours?" I asked.

"We both ate. I'll clean up so we can be on our way."

"Ok Annie, these are sure tasty." I finished and helped Annie load the horses. We mounted up and left for the Valley of the Ancients.

We traveled for seven days and came to the town the old man had put the 'x' on the map.

"Let's go in slow and wary," Annie. "Not sure what we'll find here."

We both studied the town as we went in; a store, a blacksmith shop and a cantina.

"Let's stop here" I said, "and I'll go in for a talk. Stay with the horses and I'll be right back. You stay with Annie Big Jake."

I walked in and stepped to the side letting my eyes adjust to the darkness. I saw four men at a table playing cards and a Mexican bar tender. I walked on up to the bar and asked if he had any food.

"Si senor we have beans and tortillas."

"Set up two plates and some water, be back directly."

I went back outside and told Annie we had food coming.

"Let's water the horses and go inside."

We tied up the horses and went inside to eat. When Annie walked in the men at the table heehawed about her.

"Have a seat Annie and I got to see a man about a horse."

One of the men came over to Annie and asked her to dance. She said for him to go look in the mirror, shoot the mirror and then shoot himself. The other men laughed.

He said, "That's not funny lady," and went to grab her. Big Jake flew at him and had him down on the floor with his teeth bared.

"I wouldn't move Mister," Annie said eating her dinner.

"Listen lady I was only funning. Call off your dog."

"Big Jake quit," Annie said, and Big Jake went over and sat beside her. He got off the floor and said to Annie, "Some people just can't take a joke."

I came in a few minutes later and looked around. "I miss something Annie?" I asked.

"Nope, good beans dig in."

We finished eating and went over to the store.

"Annie I forgot to ask you; any water where were going?"

"Yes," she said, "a small stream right where we'll camp."

"Good let's get what we need and leave."

We purchased a lantern, pick and more rope as well as several sacks of grain for the horses.

"You have any kegs of black powder?" I asked the clerk.

"Yes sir."

I told him, "We'll take one."

"I think we got it all," I said. "Let's load up and get down the trail."

"Ok Big Zach," she said, "were ready."

Four days later we entered the Valley of the Ancients.

We walked our horses into the Valley of the Ancients. I was a little taken back at the size. The homes on the cliff were identical to those in the Valley of the Mist.

"Big Zach," Annie said. "There is a good place to camp over there, mostly shaded and the stream is there."

I looked over the camping spot and it had most of what we needed. The spot could be defended and there was a spot to corral the horses. We got down and I let Big Jake loose. He went around sniffing the ground and I was satisfied no Indians were around. We moved farther into the area and unloaded the horses. I got some rope and tied off a large area for the horses.

"Wow," Annie said, "I like it. The horses will have plenty of room to move around and the water is right there."

First thing we did was rub down the horses and grain them. I put up a tarp for some shade and we set up camp.

"All done Big Zach," Annie said. "Isn't this place wonderful?" "Yes," I answered, "and a little bit foreboding."

"I know what you mean," replied Annie.

"First thing I would like to do Big Zach is visit my father's grave," Annie said.

"Sure Annie let's go."

We walked up a small rise and there was a large mound of stones. Annie knelt down and put her hand on the grave. She spoke for a minute and got up.

"What did you say?" I asked.

"I told him I wouldn't let Martin get away with is death. And vowed I get his revenge."

We turned back toward camp and I saw tears in Annie's eyes.

"Let's get to work," Annie said bringing over the maps to our blankets. She unrolled them and we looked at the two

Kokopelli's that were on the map of the Valley of the Ancients.

"This is strange!" she said, "I didn't notice this before, but the Kokopelli's are facing each other. The one on the left is facing right and the one on the right is facing left. I don't know if it means anything, but the ones on your shirt are the same. One facing the other the one on the left here being on the front of your shirt and the other on the back."

"Let's check out the one on the left first," I said. "Do you remember where it is?"

"Yes," she said, "it should be just over there."

We walked several hundred yards and Annie was having trouble finding it. She looked around and said, "There it is behind us." We turned and walked back. "Here it is," said Annie. "Looks identical to the map and my drawing."

I got down on my knees and studied the Kokopelli. I brushed away the dirt and felt the painting with my hand. The rock was pitted from hundred maybe thousands of years of weathering.

"Nothing stands out to me," I said to Annie. "Just looks like a painting." Annie went over and confirmed my thoughts.

"Where is the other one?" I asked Annie.

"Should be just over there," she pointed.

We walked over and Annie found it right off. I did the same thing to this one and found nothing that looked like a sign or anything to help us find the treasure. We walked back to camp and sat down on our blankets. Annie set the map in front of her and made some mental notes.

"Big Zach," she said, "there are only three signs on the map in this location. The two Kokopelli's and this sign of the sun."

"Have you ever seen this sign in the valley?" I asked her.

"Yes," she replied, "but not in this area. They are further down the valley, but they are not like this one."

She pulled out some paper and drew the sign making it larger. We both sat there looking at what she drew.

"What do you make of it Annie?"

Annie drew the sun and an oval line that dissected the sun from the far right. There was another line beneath the sun and three squiggly lines beneath the straight line.

"What do you see when you look at this Big Zach?"

"I see a sunny day and these squiggly lines could be a waterfall."

"It could be," Annie said, "but I doubt there has been a waterfall in this valley for thousands of years." She picked up her drawing and held it up to the cliff. "What if the straight line means the lip of the canyon and the squiggly lines the face of the cliffs?"

"That makes sense," I said squinting. "What about the sun and the oval line?" I asked.

"I think the oval line depicts a day of sunlight and where the sun is on the line depicts the time of day." Annie got real excited and gave me a kiss. "I think I know what this means Big Zach," she said. "According to this sign something happens just when the sun comes over the lip of the canyon." She sat back down flustered, "But I have no idea what that is."

"Annie," I said, "you are one smart lady. I knew I brought you along for a reason."

"See," she said, "I'm good at other things besides, well you know other things!" she said batting he eyes.

"Yes you are," I said, "and you're damn good at that other thing too."

We both laughed. Big Jake came over to see what was happening and barked at both of us wagging his stump of a tail.

CHAPTER 22

"Let's fix something to eat and think about this," Annie said.

"I'm for that and Big Jake looks hungry too."

"Get me some water and I'll start a fire."

Annie fixed biscuits and bacon with beans. She made a lot and we ate it all. Big Zach laid under the tarp and took a nap.

"Big Zach," Annie said, "let's go back to the Kokopelli's. Bring that canteen and a rag."

We walked over to the first Kokopelli and Annie poured water on it and scrubbed it. She poured water to rinse it off and looked at it with a magnifying glass.

"Big Zach," she said excited. "Look at this." She gave me the magnifying glass and said, "There in his eye."

I looked and to my surprise I saw a little piece of glass. "It's a piece of glass," I said.

"No it isn't Big Zach, it's a diamond. Hurry let's go look at the other one."

Annie beat me to it and poured water on it. She scrubbed and then poured more water to rinse it off. I handed her the magnifying glass and she squeaked with delight. "There's a diamond on here too Big Zach." She grabbed me and danced me around and around.

Martin got back to town and found the only dentist in town.

"Damn mister," he said, "what happen to you?"

"Never mind," he said, "can you fix me up?"

"Well," he said, "I'll have to pull eight of your teeth out. Can't fix them.

These must hurt like hell," the dentist said.

"Yes they hurt, go ahead and do it," Martin said.

"It's going to hurt mister. Take a slug of this it will deaden the pain."

"This tastes like shit, what is it anyway?"

"Its laudanum," said the dentist. "Drink the whole bottle and you won't feel a thing."

Martin slugged down the bottle and two hours later left the dentist missing eight teeth and a big hangover.

Martin weaved his way to his room and went up to his bed. He threw up and passed out face first in his mess. When Martin woke up he said to himself, "why me, why me?" and went to use the outhouse.

Several hours later and feeling a lot better he made his way down to the Mexican side of Albuquerque. He was looking for Fernando's Cantina. A place he heard was full of some very bad hombres. He walked up to the bar and ordered a tequila from a very large Mexican with bad teeth. At least he had teeth Martin thought to himself.

"Hey hombre," the bartender said. "You get kicked by a mule?" he laughed.

"Yah a mule," Martin said back to him.

"Hey gringo, you know you are in a very bad place. These men will slit your throat for a dollar."

"Oh yah," said Martin. "Which one is the worst of the bunch?"

"He sits over there with the pretty whore on his lap. His name is Jose Luis Vargas. They say he has killed twenty men with his knife."

"Just the man I'm looking for. Give me a bottle," he said and threw money on the bar.

Martin got up and walked over to his table. "Mind if I sit down and buy you a drink?" said Martin.

The Mexican bad man looked at Martin and said, "You look like shit man. What happened you get kicked by a mule in the face?" and he laughed.

"Where have I heard that one before?" Martin said under his breath. Martin dismissed the comment and asked him if he was looking for work.

"What kind of work gringo? You want me to find the mule and kill him for you?" he said laughing.

"Something like that," Martin said. "It's worth five hundred in gold to me."

The bandit pushed the whore off his lap and told Martin to follow him. "So for five hundred in gold, consider him dead."

"He has a dog I want killed too," Martin added.

"For you gringo, I throw him in for free," Jose Luis said laughing. "Where is he?" Jose Luis asked.

"In a Valley two weeks ride."

"This mule you want dead, is he alone?"

"No," Martin said. "He is with a very pretty girl."

"A girl," Jose Luis said stroking his beard. "And what is this mule doing in this valley gringo?"

"He and the girl are looking for something I want."

"What is that?" he said.

"I don't know, but whatever it is it's mine. When we get there we watch them and when they find it, I take it and you can have the girl and five hundred in gold."

"I think I like you gringo," he said. "Where is this valley?" Jose Luis asked.

"Two weeks ride north. It is called the Valley of the Ancients."

"Yes gringo, I know the place, I have been once. This man and girl are they there now?" he asked.

"No they left early this morning."

"Then we can be there before they are. I know another way there." "When can we start?" Martin asked.

"In the morning," Jose Luis said. "I will bring four men. Meet me here when the sun comes up," and he left.

Early the next morning all five of the would be killers and thieves left Albuquerque for the Valley of the Ancients. Eight days later they made camp on the rim of the valley. Martin and Jose were looking over the edge of the rim.

"Gringo, is that them? The mule and the girl?"

"Yes that's them," replied Martin.

"I also see the dog. It is a funny looking dog. I think I will have it stuffed and mounted for my hacienda," Jose Luis said cackling. "And the girl she is very pretty, I think I will keep her, she will bear me many sons." The thought of the dirty Mexican with Annie repulsed him, but what the hell, he was going to kill her anyway.

CHAPTER 23

"What they are doing down there going from rock to rock?"

"I'm not sure, but let's watch and see," said Martin.

Martin got up and went to his horse. "Here," he said, "this will help," and handed Jose Luis a telescope.

"Ah the girl is even prettier than I thought," Jose Luis said slobbering. "What do they do now gringo, dancing around?"

"I think they found something," replied Martin.

Annie stopped and said, "Big Zach I'm not positive, but I think I may know what will happen in the morning."

Big Zach looked up at the ridge of the canyon and saw a light blink. "Annie don't look, but I just saw a light from the top of the canyon. Something reflecting the sun. Maybe a gun or, I'm not sure but we got company."

"You think it's Indians?" Annie asked.

"Maybe, but I'd bet its Martin. Let's get back to camp."

Annie and I sat back down on our blankets. "What do we do Big Zach?" Annie asked.

"If it's Martin he won't do anything until we find something. If it's the Indians, they might do nothing. Or they might try to kill us just for fun. One thing I do know is we have to be on guard."

"I may be wrong, but it has something to do with the sun coming over the ridge in the morning and those diamonds. Other than that I'm not sure what will happen, but we'll know as soon as the sun comes over the lip of the canyon."

We made supper and stood guard the rest of the night.

I woke early and Big Jake came around a rock by the entrance to our camp. He stopped and licked my face wagging his stump of a tail. Annie was fixing something to eat and I smelled coffee.

"You up already?" she asked.

"Yes, must have been the coffee, sure smells good."

"It will be light in an hour and maybe another hour till the sun gets over the ridge," Annie said.

"Then we better eat and get ready for whatever may happen," I said.

"Where do you think we should be when the suns comes over the ridge?" I asked Annie.

"In front of each Kokopelli," she said.

"You take the one on the left and I'll take the one on the right and see what happens."

"It's about time," Annie said, "let's get in position."

We walked to the Kokopelli's and waited. I looked up at the ridge and the sun was just starting to emerge.

"Get ready," I told Annie. "Here it comes."

The sun peeked over the ridge and the most amazing thing happened. The sun light hit the diamond on the one I was standing next to and then the light jumped over to the one Annie was standing by. Then shot over hitting the canyon wall. It stayed for a second and blinked out.

Annie came over to me and said, "That was the most amazing thing I have ever seen."

"Let's go see what's on that cliff the light hit," I said.

We both rushed over and examined the wall. "I don't see anything Big Zach," Annie said.

"I don't either," I said, "but something must be here."

Annie brushed her hand against the stone wall and pieces came off in her hand. She brushed a little harder and more fell from the stone. She turned around and said, "Big

Zach look over to the other side of the canyon. You see anything?"

I went where Annie was standing and looked where she pointed. "Sorry Annie, but I don't see anything."

"No," she said, "but whoever is watching thinks we see something. Get excited and point with me."

I did as she asked and said, "What now?"

"Turn around and look at the wall where I brushed it with my hand and then look back here."

I turned and looked and turned back again pointing. "Let's go back to camp," Annie said, "I know where to dig."

"So what is it you think is going to happen with the Kokopelli's?" I asked Annie.

"Big Zach, the face of the rock is crumbling, but the rock itself is hard. There must be a tunnel or a cave behind the rock. The Anasazi put a false front on the rock. When it gets dark we can open it up and look inside."

Jose Luis said, "Did you see that gringo what has happened?"

"I'm not sure, but it must be a sign as to where or what they're looking for. Now they are pointing to the other side of the canyon. The Big one is getting very excited. And he is also pointing. Give me the telescope." Jose Luis handed it to him and Martin scanned the other side of the canyon. "It must be over there, but I don't see anything."

"We need to make whoever is watching think that whatever we are looking for is not here. What if we mount up and go over to the other side and start digging. Come back when it starts to get dark, make dinner, and wait for it to get dark."

"Hey gringo they are saddling their horses."

Martin went over and said, "Let's see."

The Mexican handed him the telescope and he watched them load shovels and ride to the other side. Martin handed back the telescope to the Mexican and told him to watch them; if it looked like they found something to let him know.

"Si senor," he replied.

CHAPTER 24

We loaded up the horses and left for the other side of the canyon. We both hoped that whoever was watching would think this was the treasure site. Until we had a chance to look on the other side of that rock, we would look busy digging here and there and looking disgusted, then we would finally return to camp.

"They are returning gringo," said the Mexican. "And they look tired and how you say pissed off."

"Ok," Martin said, "let me know if they do anything when they get back."

"Hey gringo," Jose Luis said. "When do we make a move?"

"Not until I tell you," said Martin. "I want whatever they are looking for and you agreed to stay until then."

"Yes I did, but it better be soon!" and he walked away.

We got back to camp, took care of the horses and made supper. The sun was just going down and we talked about what we were going to do.

"Annie if we start chipping away with the pick they will hear us," I said.

"I know, but the wall seems to be very soft, maybe we can do this with knifes and not make any noise. When we get it open we can go inside and use the lantern without anyone seeing it."

"Well its dark enough, let's sneak over there and see what we can do."

We both took our knives and the lantern over to the wall. I had Big Jake lay down and watch our backs. Annie got right to work and the wall was pretty easy to chip away. While she worked on one side I worked on the other. We had been at it for several hours when my knife went all the way through.

"Annie," I whispered, "I'm through."

Annie came over and helped with the opening I had started. The wall gave way and we pulled the rest out of the way. The opening wasn't very big and I doubted if I could get into it.

"You'll have to go in Annie."

She went into the opening and said, "Big Zach hand me the lantern." She put it in front of her and lit it. The whole cave came to light. "It's pretty big in here once you get past the opening come on in," she told me.

I squeezed through the opening and it was rather large in side. It smelled really old and damp.

"See anything?" I asked Annie. She didn't answer me. "Annie you see anything?" I said again. She still didn't answer and I walked over to her.

Standing in front of her was a golden statue about three feet high. Annie finally got her tongue to work and said, "It is the same as the statue my father found."

I was pretty stunned myself; it was beautifully carved and glistened bright as the sun in the cave. All around it were large stones and jewelry. They glittered in the light. I bent over and picked up a stone holding it in the light. It was bright red. There were others of different sizes and colors. Some were white like the eyes of the Kokopelli's.

"Look," I said and handed Annie a gold ring.

It was inscribed with the same Kokopelli as the maps. "Here's another," Annie said. "See if they fit." I put mine on and it fit pretty well. Annie's was a bit loose. "Let's get this out of here," she said, "and hide it."

I grabbed it and took it toward the door. "Douse the light Annie," I said and we went out with the statue. I took it over to where we had our out house and buried it in the sand.

I went back and Annie said, "We need to cover the hole up."

"Get a tarp and get it wet. We can roll it in the dirt and cover the hole. From up there they probably can't tell the difference."

I went back in the cave, took out my poke and filled it with as many of the stones that would fit in it. I came out and helped Annie put the tarp in place.

"Can't tell in this light for sure, but I think it's good enough to fool whoever is watching from above."

We went to our blankets and I told Annie to get some sleep, I would stand the first watch. Something told me trouble was coming and I wanted to be ready. An idea came to me, Big Jake and I both got up and went over to one of the packs. I grabbed the keg of blasting powder and put it in the cave just to the side. I could put a bullet in it and seal the cave if I needed to. I went back and sat down. I patted Big Jake on the head and waited. Annie relieved me a few hours later and then woke me for breakfast.

I didn't look at the cave, but Annie asked if the tarp looked good enough to fool whoever was watching.

"Come over and get some coffee and look yourself." I walked over and bent down looking at the cave. It almost looked real until you looked at it twice.

"Should be good enough," I said and we ate breakfast.

After we had cleaned up Big Jake alerted in his 'Indians are here' growl. I called Annie and said, "Indians."

We both looked around but couldn't see where he was watching. He turned around and took off for Annie. Just then a big Indian came around the rock and grabbed her. Big Jake leapt for the Indian, but he side stepped him and kicked him hard when he flew by. I heard him yelp and then there was silence. I got up and pulled my pistols. The Indian had a knife at Annie's throat and motioned me to throw down my guns. I threw them down and he turned Annie toward him and hit her hard in the face. Annie went down and he came at me.

CHAPTER 25

"Hey gringo, look there is an Indian; he is fighting with the big man down there."

Martin ran over and grabbed the telescope. Jose Luis joined him.

"The woman is dead," said Jose Luis. "And that Indian is going to kill the gringo."

"Don't worry Jose, if he does kill him you'll still get your money and the girl. I can see her moving. Ok let's move," said Martin and they mounted up racing to get to the camp.

The Indian came at me slashing with his knife. I pulled mine and we went around in a circle slashing and pairing. He dodged my thrust and slashed my arm and I dropped the knife. A big smile came to his face and he came forward. I dodged away from his knife several times and he finally cut me across my chest. My Buckskins took most of it, but it still hurt like hell. He came at me again and I fainted to the left, he tried to move around, but I caught him with a wicked right to his nose and he fell back and I could see blood everywhere on him. That got him mad and he came at me again. I fainted again and caught him with a left hook to his jaw and he dropped the knife and fell to his knees. I started toward him when a spear went through him. The Indian got a strange look on his face and then fell over dead.

Annie was standing holding her pistol, but was looking over my shoulder. I turned and looked, and to my surprise the old man from the village was standing on a rock. He was dressed just like a defender in the Valley of the Mist. I told Annie not to shoot and looked back, but he was gone. I rushed over to Big Jake and he was breathing. I couldn't see any wounds except a small one on his head. He had hit his head on a rock when he went down. I picked him up and took him over to the creek I put water on his head and he woke up with a start.

"Easy boy easy," I said, "you're all right just stay there a minute." I gave him some water and he perked up.

Annie came over and got on her knees by us. "He is ok Big Zach?' she said petting Big Jake.

"Yes I think he'll be fine, just needs to rest up." I took him over to our tarp and laid him under it out of the sun. "You take it easy boy and I'll be back. Annie you ok?" I said.

"Yes I'm fine. My jaw hurts a little, but I'll be fine, just so long as Big Jake is ok."

"He'll be fine," I replied. "I think we're going to have visitors in a few minutes. Make sure your pistols are loaded and get ready."

Annie looked over her pistols and I grabbed my rifle and reloads. I went over to Big Jake and put his harness on tying him to a big rock just in case he decided to help.

"Annie get behind those rocks. When they go by sneak back around and take a position you can get a shot at them without exposing yourself. I'm going to play dead and see what happens."

I grabbed the dead Indian and moved him behind some cover where they couldn't' see him. Then I removed the tarp and laid on my stomach my Colt cocked under me.

Martin and his thugs raced down the canyon to our camp site. They flew by Annie and stopped in front of where I was laying. They all dismounted and Jose said, "Where is the woman, did the Indian take her?"

I peeked through my eyelids and counted four Mexicans and Martin. Martin raced into the cave and came right back out. He went over and grabbed the lantern. Jose Luis came over to me and pushed me over. I held the Colt on him and said with a smile, "You're dead," and pulled the trigger. He flew back into his men.

Annie stepped out with both her pistols and let loose. When it was over they were all down on the ground.

"Where's Martin?" Annie asked.

"In the cave."

She started to walk over to the cave when a shot came from the cave. Annie went down and I rushed over to her pulling her to safety.

"How bad you hurt?" I asked.

"I'm fine he can't even shoot straight."

Annie had a nasty burn across her leg. I took her bandana and wrapped up her leg. I fired into the cave and another shot came our way. I grabbed up Annie and took her around to the other side of the rocks. I went over and put another round into the cave and I heard Martin cry out. I grabbed Big Jake and took him over to Annie.

"Keep a tight hold on his ears and put this in yours." I handed her some cloth and left. I went over to the horses and cut the rope. I yelled and they all went running down the canyon. I picked up my rifle and got into a position where I could see the front of the cave.

"Hey Martin," I yelled. "You see all those gems and diamonds?"

"What else was in here?" he yelled.

"A statue Martin, just like the one you killed Annie's father over."

"I want that statue or I'll kill you both and send you to hell."

I yelled back, "You first," and fired at the blasting powder.

The shot hit it and a huge explosion rocked the valley. Tons of rock and dirt fell in on the tunnel, and the earth shook violently. I got up and ran to Annie and Big Jake. They were both sitting there. Annie took the cloth from her ears and asked me if Martin was dead.

"He was sitting on that keg of powder when it went up."

She sighed and laid back her head. I grabbed up Annie and told Big Jake to come. I took her over to the creek and bathed her wound.

"You're hurt too," she said.

"Yes, but let's get you fixed up and then you can fix me up."

I got some bandages and salve from the pack and fixed Annie up. Big Jake was back to his normal self and Annie went to work on me. Most of my cuts weren't deep and I didn't need any stitches. I walked and Annie hobbled back to our blankets .She lay down with Big Jake by her side.

"I'm going to see if I can get the horses back." I said.

I told Big Jake to stay, grabbed some sugar and walked out into the valley. I could see them off a ways and whistled. Buck's ears pricked up and he came running. The other horses followed and when Buck came to me I gave him his sugar. I put the other horses back into the corral and retied the rope. I grained them heavy and went back to see Annie and Big Jake.

"I got the horses back, you feel like eating anything?" I asked.

"Not now Big Zach. Those men are getting ripe."

I pulled them all over to the cave and pushed rock down on them. They were covered, but if the coyotes wanted them after we left it was ok by me.

CHAPTER 26

I dug up the statue and put it beside Annie. "Well young lady what are you going to do with that," I pointed.

"Me?" she said, "it's half yours."

"No Annie it's all yours," I said. "If it wasn't for you we would never have found it. Your father would be proud, you are one hell of an archeologist."

Annie smiled and said, "You really mean it. It's all mine?"

"Yes young lady, it's all yours," I replied.

"Then you know what I'm going to do?"

"Nope," I answered.

"I'm going to give it to the museum at the university just like my father would have done."

"I'm proud of you Annie and you father would be too."

"What about the old man Big Zach?" Annie asked.

"I don't know what to think about him," I replied. "He was dressed just like the defenders in the Valley of the Mist. I would think he would have killed me. We were the ones taking the statue. But he killed the Indian." "One of the reasons they left was marauding Indians. It was like he was defending us," Annie said.

"Maybe he saw the rings," I said. "But I guess we may never know."

"Annie," I said, "let's go. We're loading up and leaving for Santa Fe right now."

I had everything packed and loaded and we left the Valley of the Ancients. Ten days later we walked into Santa Fe.

"What a beautiful little town," she said.

"I know," I said, "you love the southwestern style and the Mexican people."

"You know me too well Big Zach." We both laughed.

We walked through town and came to a livery. We got down and a young Mexican boy greeted us. "Welcome to Santa Fe, my name is Eduardo. Do you wish to stable your horse's senor?"

"Yes all four."

"How long may I ask?"

I looked at Annie and said, "Three or four days." She smiled and I said, "How much?"

"Ten cents a day, twenty with grain."

"Ok Eduardo with grain."

"Follow me please," he said. He took us to some nice stalls in the back of the livery. "I will even rub them down senor."

I said, "Those two ok, but these two are a bit troublesome to strangers. We'll rub these down ourselves."

"Say Eduardo," asked Annie, "is there a good hotel in town?"

"Yes senorita it is just down the street. It is called the Santa Fe. My cousin is the manager. Say I sent you please."

"Ok Eduardo I will."

"Do you have any place our packs will be safe?" I asked.

"Yes senor in there. I keep it locked and we have never lost anything."

"Ok, let's put these in there." I picked up the packs and followed Eduardo into the room.

I grabbed my rifle and the statue and Annie grabbed her bag and the maps. We went down to the hotel and checked in.

"Eduardo sent us," Annie said.

"Ah," he said, "my cousin. Welcome to the Hotel Santa Fe. My name is Rodrigo how can I help you?"

"One room and a two hot baths."

"For how long senor?"

"Four days," said Annie, butting in.

"Very well, is your perro staying with us too?" he asked.

"Yes," I said, "him too."

"Very good then I will put you on the ground floor. This room opens into our garden, you will like it very much."

He handed us the keys and said, "Right this way." He took us to the room and said, "Your baths will be ready in one hour. I will come get you."

"Thanks," we both said and went inside.

Annie threw herself on the bed again and said, "Wake me in a month or when our baths are ready."

I unpacked and opened the doors to the garden. The trees and the flowers were in bloom and it was like heaven.

"You're missing this," I said to Annie.

She got up and walked out the door. "I'm in heaven!" she said, "what a beautiful garden." She walked around and smelled the flowers. "I want a place just like this when I grow up," she said.

We both laughed.

Rodrigo came to the door a few minutes later and said, "Your baths are ready senor and senorita."

We grabbed our clothes, my rifle and the statue and followed him into a large room with two steaming baths.

"I will let you bathe," and he left.

I walked over and locked the door. When I turned around Annie was already in. I stripped and got in myself. We stayed for over an hour and when I got out I gave Big Jake his bath.

CHAPTER 27

We dressed and went back to our room. I opened the garden doors and let the fresh air and smell into our room.

"Annie I will be right back. Big Jake stay," and I left the room.

I went to see Rodrigo and asked if he could arrange dinner for us out in the garden. He winked and I placed our order.

"Say eight o'clock."

"Yes senor, and I will have the lanterns lit. It is very lovely."

"Could you also get some music?"

"Si senor, my cousin has a mariachi band."

"Perfect," I said. I thanked him and went back to our room.

Several hours went by and Annie noticed several young boys setting up table and chairs in the garden.

"Annie," I asked, "do you still have that beautiful dress you purchased?"

"Yes Big Zach, but why?"

"Humor me and put it on." She found the dress and changed into it. "You're a beautiful woman Annie." I grabbed her hand and walked her out into the garden.

"Is this for us?" she smiled.

"Yes it is," I replied. I pulled out her chair and the musicians came out. Annie had tears in her eyes. It was a beautiful evening with a beautiful lady.

We spent the next four days in Santa Fe just enjoying the sites and relaxing. Annie came to me and said she wanted to go home. We packed up the next day and left for St. Louis. I found an easier and less dangerous route home. It was, at least for the first half of the journey.

We traveled pretty fast making good time. Our horses were in great shape and the weather was mild. The next day we got about ten miles when we saw smoke in the distance.

"What do you make of it?" Annie asked me.

"Too much smoke for anything but a house or barn," I said. "Let's go see, and we'll take it slow and careful, I smell Indians."

I untied Big Jake and told him to trail and stay close. If there were Indians around I wanted to know. We got closer and Big Jake alerted with his low 'Indian's are here' growl. We stopped short of a small rise and I got down pulling my rifle.

"Annie," I said, looking around. "Let's take a look."

We got down and I told big Jake to crawl with us and we all stuck our heads over the rise. Big Jake growled again and I told him to quit.

"Damn Big Zack," Annie said. "Looks like it was a nice ranch house and barn."

We looked down and both structures were completely destroyed by fire. "I wonder if anyone is alive?" asked Annie.

I took my telescope and scanned the area. "See anything Big Zach?" Annie asked.

"Nobody down there and no Indians." Just then Big Jake turned and bolted for the horses. When we turned around two Indians jumped on our horses and tried to run. Big Jake leaped for the one on Annie's horse Thunder and knocked him off. We both got up pulled our pistols and went after them. The one Big Jake had was screaming and kicking at him. He managed to kick Big Jake off and got up running. He made it about five steps and Big Jake caught him by the back of the leg. The Indian screamed and went down. He turned over to fight the dog but Big Jake had moved to his head. The Indian kicked a few times and lay still. Big Jake tore out his throat. I told Big Jake to quit and he returned to me. I looked back at Annie and she was aiming at the Indian on Buck. I told Annie not to fire and whistled for Buck. He put on the brakes and the Indian flew over his head. The Indian jumped up and started running with Buck after him. The Indian ran and dodged Buck for a few minutes. Buck finally caught him and took a big chunk out of his shoulder. The Indian went down and Buck stomped him to death. I looked at Annie and she grabbed her face, looking away. I whistled for Buck and he came back running. When I caught him I settled him down and reached for a piece of sugar in my saddle bag. I gave him the sugar and praised him for coming to me.

"You all right Annie?" I, asked.

"Yes," she said, "it's just that I... had never seen anything like that before."

"We need to get out of here," I said. "There may be more around."

We mounted up and I told Big Jake to trail. We found some cover and rode to the other side of the burning ranch. We dismounted and we found a place to view the ranch house. I scanned the area again and didn't see anything.

"We've got to go down there and see if anyone survived," Annie said.

"I know," I replied, "and we better do it fast before those Indians we killed get missed."

I started to get up when Big Jake alerted. I looked where he was looking and a small cloud of dust was coming toward the ranch house. I looked through the telescope and saw a very small horse heading toward the ranch house.

"What is it Big Zach?" Annie asked.

"Looks like a small horse to me. Here you take a look," and I handed Annie the telescope.

"Oh no," said Annie.

"What?" I asked.

"It stopped by a horse down by the corral. Must be its mother."

Annie handed back the telescope and I took another look.

I got up and said to Annie, "Let's get down there but go slow."

When we got to the ranch house there was nothing left but burnt out cinders. I told Big Jake to stay and went in to look around. When I came out Annie had the little colt tied up and I went over to have a look.

"Isn't he just the cutest little thing?" Annie said.

"He is nice looking," I said, checking him over. "See here, he has rope burns on his neck. He must have got loose from the Indians. That's another reason to get out of here. No one made it through the fire," I said.

Annie looked at me and I said, "Bring him along." She smiled and we got out of there.

We didn't stop until it got nearly dark.

"We better have a cold camp tonight," I said. "Let's not make it easy for those Indians to find us."

"You think they're looking for us?"

"When they find their dead friends they will," I replied. "Let's get some salve on the little guy's neck."

After we doctored up the colt, Annie gave him some grain.

We made camp and Annie lay beside me. "What kind of Indians were they Big Zach?" she asked.

"Apaches," I answered. "Mean and deadly."

We took turns throughout the night watching for trouble. Annie came over to me at first light and asked if I had seen anything.

"No, but that doesn't mean they're not out there. If they get close Big Jake will let us know."

"Can I make breakfast then?" Annie asked.

I said, "Go ahead. I'll keep watch."

Annie cooked and we ate pretty fast and packed up to leave. I took the lead and told Big Jake to trail.

Sometime that afternoon we cut a trail and Big Jake stopped to smell around. He looked up at me and I got down and walked over to him. "What did you find boy?" I said stroking his head.

He growled in his low growl and I knew Indians were close by. The tracks were from six unshod horses and one with shoes. Annie came up and asked what we had found.

"Indians," I said. "I count seven horses, maybe two or three hours old. There going the way we are so we better keep on our toes."

We remounted and rode off easy.

It was getting dark and we decided to keep going to see if we could get farther away from the Indians. We were riding down an arroyo several hours later when Big Jake alerted. I told Annie to stay where she was and got down to see where Big Jake was looking. I sighted down the way he was looking and we both went up the side to have a look.

We were looking directly into the Apache camp. They had a small fire going and I counted six of them. There was one missing. I scanned the camp again and then I saw the seventh. It was a young white woman tied by her hands to a tree. They were passing some bottles back and forth. I called Big Jake and went back to Annie.

"Indian camp over there," I whispered.

Annie looked at me and said, "What else Big Zach?"

"There's a young white woman tied to a tree. Must be from the ranch they raided."

I mounted up and motioned Annie to follow. I found a nice place to hide the horses and we stopped. We both got down and I whispered to her. "There are six of them and their drinking pretty heavy."

"Big Zach, we are going to help her aren't we?" Annie asked.

"Yes we are, so let's make a plan. It's going to take all of us to do this. Here's what I have in mind. We give them time to get good and drunk. There is some good cover all around the camp."

We waited a few more hours and crept on their camp. We both hid behind some rocks and looked the camp over. The girl was completely naked, but didn't look too beat up.

I whispered to Annie, "If we don't kill them all they will come after us. You take Big Jake and get close to the girl. When you are ready wave to me. I'll be over there."

Annie nodded and we both snuck away. I got into position and Annie waved to me. I was about to make a move when an Indian got up and came over by me. He lifted up his breech cloth and relieved himself. When he turned to go back I jumped up covering his mouth and slit his throat. Almost no sound came out of him. I dragged him back into the bushes and went back to my spot.

There were two sleeping by themselves and I crawled toward them. When I got to them one raised up and threw up all over himself. It smelled bad. I put my hand over his mouth and sliced my knife across his throat. I looked over and Annie was cutting the girls bonds. The other one woke up just as I turned and let out a blood gurgling scream. The whole camp woke up and I put my knife in his heart. Two of them saw Annie with the girl and one came after me. I pulled my knife from the dead Indian and was tackled by the one coming after me. He knocked me back and the knife flew from hand. He jumped on me and drew his knife. I caught his hand before he could stick me and used my leg to throw him over my head. I jumped up and he came at me again.

He was game and knew how to wrestle. He swept my legs and I landed on the bottom with him trying to stick me again. I let go of his left hand and grabbed his right fist in my hand. I squeezed as hard as I could and heard several bones break. He yelled and released the knife. I got up and hit him hard on the chin. He went down like a poll axed steer and I stuck the knife in his heart. I looked up, Annie and the girl were gone. So was the last Indian. Big Jake had one down and was tearing him apart. I ran over to Big Jake and told him to quit.

"Big Jake, find Annie," I told him. He sniffed by the tree and took off toward the horses. I ran after him and lost him in the dark. A few seconds later I heard a gunshot and found the Indian dead at Annie's feet with Big Jake tearing him apart. I told Big Jake to quit and went to Annie.

"You ok?" I asked.

"Yes, I am now. Big Jake distracted him long enough for me to shoot him."

The girl was just standing here. The look in her eyes said everything. I grabbed her and sat her down. She didn't care if I saw her naked or not. "Annie some water and something to cover her up." I said.

I looked the girl in the face and told her it was all over and she was going to be alright. Annie came over and put a blanket around her. Annie handed her the canteen and she guzzled the water. I took it away and told her to go slow, we have all you want, and gave it back to her. She drank slower and looked me in the eyes. I saw a very pretty girl maybe fifteen or so. She lowered her head and broke down crying. I got up and Annie comforted her.

"We need to get out of here Annie," I said. "Can you get her some clothes and get ready to travel."

Annie went and got her some clothes and helped her to get dressed.

"She'll have to ride with you Annie," I said and I helped her up behind Annie.

I tied on Big Jake, mounted and we left. It was close to sunrise when I found a suitable place to defend and we stopped. I got down from Buck and helped the girl from Annie's horse. I took her over to a spot and I told her to stay put and be quiet. Annie and I set up camp and I got some coffee on the boil.

I looked at the girl and asked her name.

"Sunny," she said, "Sunny Harper."

"Well Sunny, I'm Big Zach and this is Annie. Oh, and that's is Big Jake. Was that your family's ranch we saw burned a ways back?' I asked.

She nodded and a tear came to her eye.

"Can you tell us what happened?" I asked.

She nodded and told us the story. "They came early in the morning when we'd just finished eating breakfast. I went out to feed the horses and they grabbed me. I saw it all. They broke open the door and four or five went in. I heard my mom screaming and then silence. They came out with the whiskey and set fire to the house and barns. They killed all the livestock except the colt and took me with them. The first night they got drunk and did very bad things to me. Over and over again. I just wanted to die. The second night they did the same thing. I hoped and prayed they would kill me. Then you rescued me but I think I still want to die."

"Why Sunny?" I asked.

"I heard how white folks treat woman who have been raped by savages. My ma said it was a fate worse than death."

Annie stepped over and said to Sunny, "Listen to me Sunny you are going to be fine and no one needs to know what happened. Big Zach and I will never tell. Do you have any kin Sunny?" Annie asked.

"Yes," she said, "in Bent Creek."

"Where is that?" I asked.

"Maybe three days from here east. My mom's sister lives there with her family."

Annie grabbed her and stood her up. "Listen to me Sunny and listen good. Your ma was partially right. There are some mean and nasty people out there that would use this against you. So from now, right now. This never happened. You tell them when it happened you hid out until we came along. We found you hiding in the trees. Won't no one even think otherwise as long as you don't tell them. You got it?"

"Yes Annie I hear you."

"Then get up and help me make breakfast. Your part of us now."

She smiled and got up to help Annie. "Can I ask what kind of a dog you have Big Zach."

"He's a Bouvier Des Flandres."

"A Bouvier des Flandres," she said back. "Never heard of such a dog," she said.

"No not many people have. They come from Europe."

"I saw him fight those Indians. He was very brave."

Annie called Big Jake over and he licked Sunny's face. "Big Jake," Annie said, "meet Sunny Harper" and he stuck out his paw.

Sunny shook it and said, "Nice to meet you Big Jake." She laughed and gave him a hug.

We stayed the day and got caught up on our sleep. When it got dark we loaded up and left for Bent Creek.

"Hey Sunny," I asked, "What's the colt's name?"

"Didn't name him yet. My Pa said not too. Might get too attached to him and it would hurt more when we sold him."

"That's ok Sunny," I said.

We arrived in Bent Creek the next morning. It was a small town with a store, several saloons and a hotel. I went up to a man and said, "Is there law here?"

The man pointed to a little shack on the corner. We rode over and I got down. "Where is your kin Sunny?" Annie asked.

"They own the hotel."

Just then a woman came running over, "Sunny, Sunny are you alright?"

"Yes Aunt Ginny. But Ma and Pa were killed by the Indians."

"Oh no!" Aunt Ginny said. "Come with me you sweet child," and she took Sunny to the hotel.

I tied up the horses and let Big Jake down. "Let's go see the law," I said looking at Annie. She nodded and we went in.

There was a very young man with a star pinned to his shirt.

"You the law?" I asked.

"Yes I'm Tom Bent, what can I do for you?"

"We found Sunny Harper at her burned out farm. The Indians killed her Ma and Pa and we found her hiding in the trees. Her Aunt just took her to the hotel."

"Oh no." he said. "They were really nice folks. The kind you want as neighbors. Was Sunny hurt?" he asked.

"Nope," said Annie, "she is just fine."

He seemed relieved. The door opened and Sunny came in mostly cleaned up. "Hi Tom," she said.

Annie and I saw the Sheriff looking at Sunny, and Sunny looking at him. Annie winked at me. Sunny turned and looked at us.

"I wanted to thank you before you left," she said. "You are real special to me."

"We think you're pretty special too," Annie replied. "Sheriff you take good care of her won't you?" Annie said.

He looked at Sunny and said, "Yes ma'am I will."

"What do you want to do with the colt?" I asked.

"He's yours Annie. For saving me."

"You sure?" Annie said.

"Yes, and when you look at him remember me."

"All right Sunny we will," and Annie hugged her.

"We have to be leaving," I said.

We said our goodbyes and hit the trail. Two weeks later we arrived back in St. Louis.

"It's good to be back," said Annie.

"Yes," I said, "but were not home yet. I wonder if Efren is still in business?"

"I hope so," Annie said, "I plan on giving him the colt." Annie looked at me spurred her horse and said, "Let's go see Efren."

We stopped in front of Efren's Livery several hours later. We dismounted and I let Big Jake down. "Go find Efren," I said, and he bolted through the doors. Several minutes later Big Jake came back followed by the prettiest Bouvier puppy you have ever seen. Annie bent down and scooped it up into her arms. The little thing squirmed, wiggled and carried on licking Annie's face.

Just then Efren came around the corner. "Well Howdy you two," he said shaking both our hands. "You made it back in one piece," he said.

Annie laughed. "Yes we did, but it wasn't for a lack of trying." We all had a good laugh.

"I see you met Sheba," Efren said.

"Yes," answered Annie, "and she is just the cutest thing. I love her already Efren."

I looked at Efren and said "Sheba".

Well it seemed only fitting us having the queen here. He pointed to Annie. Annie howled with laughter and I just shook my head.

"Where did you get her?" Annie asked.

"I'll tell you all about it, but let's get the horses taken care of and I want to hear all about your trip."

We settled the horses in and put the packs in Efren's locked room. Efren didn't say anything but he looked at the colt.

"What you got there?" said Efren looking at the bag I had the statue in. "Nothing much," I said and Annie laughed.

"Oh yah nothing much Efren," Annie giggled.

"Well come on in the office and take a load off," Efren offered.

When Efren settled into his chair Sheba jumped up and lay in his lap.

"I see she kind of favors you," I said to Efren smiling.

"How old is she?" Annie laughed.

"Six months today," Efren replied proudly.

"Efren what kind of dog is she?" I asked smirking.

"She's a Bouvier des Flandres you lunk head. Don't you even know what kind of dog you have?"

Annie and I laughed until we cried.

"What about the colt?" Efren asked.

"He's not for sale," said Annie.

"Well let's hear about your trip," quipped Efren.

"You first," said Annie.

"Where and how did you get Sheba?"

"Well," Efren said, "it started with an old sea captain friend of mine. He was going to England and then on to Antwerp. That's in Belgium in case you didn't know," Efren chided. "I asked him to see about getting me a female puppy and well here she is. I was hoping Big Zach when you have some time and if you're around for a while you might help me train Sheba?"

"It would be my pleasure Efren," I said.

"And maybe a few years down the road we could have some pups?" Efren asked.

"What do you think Big Jake?" I asked.

Big Jake barked and Sheba jumped off Efren's lap and tackled him. They both took off out the door playing in the hay.

"What about the colt?" he asked again.

Annie replied, "He's not for sale."

CHAPTER 28

"Ok you two it's your turn," Efren said. I pulled out the statue and sat it on Efren's desk. "What in the hell is that?" he struggled to say.

"It's a solid gold statue of the Anasazi Sun God," Annie replied.

"My word can I heft it?" he asked.

"Sure Efren," I said.

"Must weigh near twenty five pounds. Ok you two, what happened and how did you get this?" Efren asked.

We told him the whole story and he just sat there until the end.

"You two were real lucky to get back with skin," Efren said.

"It wasn't luck Efren we had Big Zach." said Annie. We all laughed and I told Efren we needed to get the statue to Mr. Goldman's bank.

"Can I leave Big Jake with you?" I asked. "I don't think the hotel will let us have him there, and besides I think he wants to stay with Sheba." We looked over and they were laying on the floor, Sheba had her head over Big Jake's legs sleeping.

"Isn't that cute," said Annie.

"We'll be here, now you go and I'll see you later."

I hefted the statue and we got a cabbie to Mr. Goldman's bank.

"Hey you two what about the colt?" Efren yelled as we left.

"You sure got Efren going Annie," I said.

"I know," she replied, "isn't this fun," and we both laughed.

When we arrived at the bank I paid the cabbie and we walked up the steps to the bank. Barney still worked there and he opened the door for us.

"Good day to you Mr. Taylor and Miss Stillwell. I sent word to Mr. Goldman, he will be with you in a moment, please have a seat."

Mr. Goldman came out of his office as we were walking over to take a seat.

"Big Zack and Miss Stillwell so nice to see you. Please come in my office." We entered and sat down in front of his desk. "It's been a long time. What have you two been up to?"

I put the bag on his desk and let the sack fall. Mr. Goldman's eyes got big around and he started choking. Annie poured him a glass of water. He drank it never taking his eyes off the statue.

When he composed himself he said, "Where on earth did you get this?" Annie and I had rehearsed a story on our way over and told it to him.

"I didn't know you were an archeologist," he said to Annie.

"Yes, I have a degree from the University of Chicago."

"An amazing story."

"Yes Mr. Goldman, and we need you to keep it a secret until Annie announces it to the world."

"Yes, yes," he said, "I will keep our conversation in strict confidence. What is it you want from me?" he asked.

"We'd like to keep it in your vault until we figure out how to move it to Chicago," Annie answered.

"I can do that. We have a special place in the vault for such valuables that only I have access to."

"Thank you so much Mr. Goldman," Annie said.

"Now would you like an update on your finances Annie and Big Zach?" "Sure," I said, "Annie's first."

He told Annie he had sold both her properties and deposited the money into her account. He scribbled an amount on a piece of paper and handed it to her.

"My Mr. Goldman!" Annie said.

"Are you pleased Miss. Stillwell?"

"Very," Annie replied.

"Now you Big Zach. Your portfolio like mine keeps growing. You're close to one hundred thousand dollars. That makes you a very rich man."

"I suppose," I said, "but money can't buy you love." Mr. Goldman and Annie laughed.

"Annie your goods are still in my warehouse. Whenever you want them just let me know." He stood and shook both our hands.

"Annie," I said, "can I talk with Mr. Goldman a minute in private."

"Sure Big Zach, I'll wait outside." Annie left and I sat back down.

"What is it Big Zach?" Mr. Goldman said.

"I have something here I need you sell for me, and I'm not sure you're the one to talk to, but have a look." I pulled my poke out of my shirt and spill it on his desk.

"My word Big Zach," he said. He picked one up and examined it under a funny eye glass. He put it down and picked up another one.

"Do you know what you have here?" he asked. "All of these are worth millions. This stone alone may be worth two hundred to three thousand alone."

"Can you help me?" I asked.

"Yes Big Zach I can. My family owns the largest diamond brokerage in New York. What would you like to do?"

"Sell them," I said, "and put half the money in each of our accounts. Except this one." I picked up a large green stone and put it back in my poke.

"The usual twenty percent fee sound fair?"

"Yes Mr. Goldman, you are more than fair. Annie doesn't know I have these so can you keep it quiet. I'd like to tell her myself."

"Yes Big Zach I can do that."

"How much do you think a man needs to live a moderate life for the rest of his years?"

"I'd say two hundred thousand would be enough to live a fairly upscale life."

"Then when you sell them put that amount away so if I decide to quit roaming I can settle down without a worry."

"Ok Big Zach I will take care of it for you. Where can I find you if I need to talk to you."

"Well we haven't got a place yet. I was hoping you could recommend a hotel not too expensive."

"May I recommend the Hotel Belvedere? It is right down the street and a dear friend of mine owns it."

"What could you do about letting me have my dog while we stay there?"

"I can arrange it. Give me an hour and then check in."

I thanked Mr. Goldman and shook his hand again. I walked out and took Annie's arm. "What's so secret Big Zach?" she said.

"It's a surprise Annie, I think you'll like."

We walked out of the bank and I hailed a cabbie.

"I don't know about you, but I think we both need some new clothes." "You got that right," Annie replied.

"Mr. Goldman is getting us set up in a hotel not far from here. We will have to be discreet, but we can get adjoining rooms."

"Yes, civilization!" Annie said.

CHAPTER 29

We spent the rest of the day shopping from store to store. We must have had fifteen packages and we both changed into new clothes.

"I really need a bath," Annie said.

"Me too. Let's go get Big Jake and our other stuff and get checked in."

The cab took us to Efren's and I took a few minutes to tell him where we would be. I told him the hotel let me have Big Jake and we would see him later.

"Wait one minute," said Efren. "What about the colt?"

"What about him Efren?" Annie asked.

"Well where did you get him?"

"That's a long story," Annie said.

"Ok, but what you going to do with him?" asked Efren.

"I don't know," said Annie. "He isn't worth much."

"What do you mean he's not worth much?" said Efren.

"He's just a bunch of bones we picked up in the trail."

"Now wait just a minute Annie," Efren said. "That colt's got some fine breeding in him."

"You think so Efren?" Annie quipped.

"Why sure I do," replied Efren.

"What do you think he's worth Efren?" Annie asked.

"Say maybe twenty five dollars."

"I don't know Efren. What do you think Big Zach?" Annie asked.

"He's worth a bit more than that I think," I replied.

"Well how much you thinking Annie?" asked Efren.

"How about two hundred dollars?" replied Annie?

"Two hundred dollars!" yelled Efren.

"You said he had some fine breeding," said Annie.

"Yes, but two hundred dollars."

"It's ok Efren we can sell him to someone else," said Annie.

"Now just hold on there Annie," Efren said.

I couldn't hold it any longer and I burst out laughing. Annie followed and we laughed and laughed. Efren stood there with his hands up.

"I'm sorry," said Annie between laughs. "We were just having some fun with you. We got the colt to give you Efren."

"You did?" said Efren.

"Yes," I said, "he's yours."

Efren got a smile on his face and told us get out of there. We said goodbye, Annie grabbed our bags and we headed laughing to the Hotel Belvedere.

We stopped out front of the hotel and a man in a funny hat opened the carriage door. Annie stepped down and told Big Jake to come.

"Are you staying with us?" he asked.

Annie said, "Yes," and could they bring all the packages up to her room. I went up to the counter and was greeted by a friendly man with a very long mustache.

"Welcome to the Hotel Belvedere."

 "Your name please?"

"Zach Taylor." I replied.

"Oh Mr. Taylor and Miss Stillwell. Yes we were expecting you."

"We want two rooms adjoining," I said.

"Certainly," the clerk said, and gave the keys to the bellhop.

"Take Mr. Taylor and Miss Stillwell to their rooms. If you need anything please let us know."

I leaned over to him and said, "We need baths."

"Yes Mr. Taylor, the baths are at the end of the hall. There is hot water ready whenever you are."

The bellhop took us to an elevator. Big Jake would not get in so I asked what floor the room was on. "Third floor room 312," said the bellhop, and me and Big Jake hoofed it up the stairs.

When we got to the third floor the bellhop was opening Annie's door. She winked at me and went in. The bellhop came over and let us in. Two other bellhops showed up with the packages and Annie said to put them in her room. She handed one some money and they left. I opened the door to Annie's room only to see another door.

Annie opened it and said, "Big Zach I'll race you to the bath."

I called Big Jake and we went out her door and down the hall. They were separate rooms. "See you in an hour," I said and we both closed and locked our doors.

It was close to an hour before me and Big Jake were clean enough to enter society again. I opened our door and locked it behind me. Annie came through the adjoining door and plopped down on the bed.

"We made it back alive Big Zach," Annie said.

"Yes we did," I replied. "What's it feel like not to have pistol within easy reach?"

Annie said, "I don't know," and put her pistol on the night stand. I laughed and Annie joined me.

"I don't feel like going out Big Zach. When we get hungry we can order room service."

"Fine with me," I replied. I plopped down on the bed next to Annie and Big Jake jumped and lay between us. Annie was petting Big Jake and the room was quiet for a few minutes.

"Big Zach," she said. "What's next for us?"

"I don't know Annie, but I know what is next for you. "

"What would that be Big Zach?" she said seriously.

"Remember when you said that whoever made this discovery would be rich and famous?"

"Famous maybe a little for a while, but rich? What Mr. Goldman got for the house and dress shop was nice, but rich? Far from it."

"What is it you'd like to do then Annie?"

"I think I'd like to teach. Maybe I could get a job at one of the local universities. Or try my hand at beaver trapping."

I laughed and said that wouldn't work as all the beaver pelts would have bullet holes in their ass. She jumped on me and we kissed.

"Big Zach," she said, "you never told me how you got Big Jake."

"No I guess I didn't. I've never told this story to anyone before."

"Is it something you can share?" she asked.

"Sure Annie it's a bit long, but if you want to hear."

"Yes Big Zach I want to hear."

So I told Annie Big Jake's story.

It was 1845 in a place near the Snake River in Idaho territory. We mountain men had what they called a rendezvous. It happens each spring at different locations. I had wintered in the mountains and had a nice bunch of beaver plews. So I went on down to rendezvous to sell them and replenish for the following season. When I arrived the place was like a party. Men were drinking and playing all kinds of games. There was even an Indian camp with several different tribes. They came and sold their pelts and their woman made buckskin clothes for the trappers. Some sold their women to the trappers.

Men came from the big cities and set up tents to sell their whiskey and whores. Some set up stores so the trappers could buy what they needed for the next season. Some even had gambling. They would buy the pelts and get the trappers to spend their money. The prices they charged were double what the stuff was worth, but the trapper's didn't care. They spent all their money on woman, drink and supplies, and for two weeks they partied. The camp barely slept. If the men weren't sleeping off hangovers they were drinking or gambling. Most were broke when they left rendezvous. A lot of fights broke out between the trappers. Whiskey can do that to men. Gives them a surely side. When it was over they shook hands and got drunk together.

CHAPTER 30

They all liked to play cards and one game in particular. It was called 'euchre'. I had played a few times in the past and wasn't very good at it. They also had tomahawk and knife throwing contests, but it seemed their favorites were fighting and running contests. I didn't drink much, and besides the whiskey that the store owners sold had all kinds of stuff in it besides whiskey. Some even had rattlesnake heads. They said it gave the whiskey a kick. That's why you hear it called snakehead whiskey. I could sell my pelts for a lot more money in St. Louis, but it was a long way there and a long way back. So I got the best price I could and found me a place to camp.

I watched the games and decided to take part in the fighting matches. I was a pretty big kid, six foot four inches tall and weighed two hundred and forty pounds. And I had plenty of muscle on every inch of it.

When I was living at the orphanage a big black Negro lived there too. He worked around the place for food and board. His name was Abu and he said he was a Mandingo warrior. I had no idea what that was, but the warrior part intrigued me. He use to talk to me about Africa and his home, but the fighting he did as a warrior was what I wanted to hear about. We went from storytelling to him showing me how to fight. We use to practice every night and he showed me a lot things. He even showed me boxing skills. How he knew how to box I never knew.

This went on for several years and finally he told me I had learned all he knew. We still practiced on and off for a time until the nuns made him stop. I was very disappointed and soon after, the nuns gave me food some clothes, a little money and said to go with God.

I was more than ready to test my skills against these mountain men. They were known for their fighting skills and use of weapons. It was a winner take all. So I put up the ten dollars and had my first fight. The man I was against was bigger than I was, and I was big. The match got started and we pawed at each other in a circle. He finally made a move and I tripped him. He fell hard and the crowd cheered. He got back up and came at me running. I side stepped him and tripped him again. The crowd noise was loud and most were cheering for him to win. He got back up and this time he came at me slow. We circled and I'd faint here and there trying to get an opening. He did the same and finally I saw one and hit him a clean one on the jaw. He stood there for a second and fell on his face out cold. The crowd cheered and patted me on the back. I stepped away for a minute to rest up. I saw a lot of side betting going on and decided to see what my odds were. I walked up to a French man who was taking bets.

"Mon ami," he said, "you are ten to one."

So I did a bit of figuring and put down one hundred dollars. If I won I would get one thousand, but I really didn't think I would win. I was called back into the circle and my next opponent was an older man. I had seen him around and most of the trappers left him alone. I figured for a reason. He was probably a mean son of a bitch. The match started and we came to the center each sizing up each other. He would faint and I would just stand there. He played like he fainted, but threw a right hand at me. I ducked, grabbed his arm and threw him over my back.

The crowd went wild and he got up dusted himself off and we circled each other. I fainted a punch and he hit me

135

solid on the chin, I staggered back and shook my head to clear it. The old man could hit. I went back in at him and he hit me again. He staggered me again and I went back in. He came at me again and I slipped the punch catching him on the side of his head, he went down and the crowd went wild. He got up and I could tell he was pissed off. He came at me throwing lefts and rights. I blocked most of them and then he hit me hard and I went down. I got right back up and we met in the middle of the circle. He put out a hand and I clenched his. He put out another and I clenched the other hand. We stood there for a few minutes and he head butted me, I saw stars and he tried again. I turned his hands upside down and put all my strength in pushing his wrist the way they weren't meant to go. He was trying to turn his hands, but I just kept up the pressure. He had finally had enough and said, "I quit!"

I let him go and he shook my hand.

I stepped away and I heard the referee say, "One match to go."

I went over and poured water on myself and didn't even watch the match. It didn't last very long and I was called back into the ring.

"This is it men, a fight to the finish, winner takes all. Ok you two," he said. "Fight!"

I probably should have watched the fights more closely because this guy was a brute. He had arms the size of my legs and towered over me. I guess he weighed near three hundred pounds. I couldn't let this monster get a hold of me or I was done for it. So I danced around him. Waiting for an opening. He was so slow I hit him repeatedly with some good shots to his face. I slipped away again and got behind him. I hit him in the kidneys several times hard and he winced. I kept on dancing and he kept on trying to catch me.

I hit him again hard on the chin and he staggered back. The crowd was deafening. He came at me again and our feet got tangled together. He managed to grab me in a bear hug and was squeezing the life out of me. Each time I tried to inhale he squeezed harder and I was running out of breath. I remembered a move the old Negro warrior had taught me and slapped both his ears hard. His grip lessoned and I was able to take a breath. He squeezed harder and I slapped both his ears again with all I had. It worked and he let me go clamping his hands on his ears. I got my breath and ran as fast as I could and put both feet in his gut. He went backwards and took half the crowd with him. I stood in the ring and waited for him to get up.

The crowd picked him up and moved him back into the circle. He came at me again, but he was hurt and tired. I side stepped him again and hit him hard in his left ear, he howled in pain and went down on a knee holding his ear. I walked up and hit hard in the other ear and followed with an uppercut. He looked up at the sky and fell backwards out cold. The crowd cheered me and put me on their shoulders carrying me around the circle. I managed to get down and the crowd slowly left to get drunk. The referee came over and paid me the money, it was two hundred dollars. I went to get my money from the French man and he was nowhere to be seen. I looked all over and finally found him in one of the tents.

"Where's my money?" I said to him. The tent got real quiet.

"What money Monsieur are you talking about?"

"The hundred dollars I bet on myself at ten to one odds."

"You never bet on yourself," he said.

"I did and you know it," I said.

Someone spoke up and said, "Pay him Frenchie I heard him bet on himself and you told him ten to one." It was the old man I had beaten earlier.

The Frenchie said, "You are mistaken mon ami, he did not bet on himself."

The old man drew is knife and said, "Pay him Frenchie or I'll carve out your liver."

The Frenchie backed off and said, "Of course I will pay him. Come with me to my tent and I'll pay you." I followed him to his tent and was met by a big black dog. "Mon ami," he said, "sit down please."

I sat and the dog came over to me. He was a breed I had never seen before.

"Say Frenchie, what kind of a dog is this?" I asked.

"It is a Bouvier Des Flandres. He comes from Belgium by way of France. Do you like him?" he asked.

"Yes," I said, "he is very nice. Now where is my money?"

"I tell you what," he said, "you take the dog and we will call it even."

"No dog is worth a thousand dollars," I said.

He looked at me and said, "This one is." And I could tell he meant what he said.

"What makes this dog worth that much money?" I asked.

"He hates Injuns and can smell one five miles away. He is also trained to fight."

"Fight how?" I asked.

"He is trained to fight people, but mostly Injuns. He is also very smart. He can do many things."

"Name ten," I said.

"He can retrieve any item I tell him to."

"Show me," I said.

He told the dog to bring and pointed to his hat. The dog got up and brought it to him. "See my friend he can bring anything you tell him to."

"What else?" I said.

"He not only knows his commands by voice, but by hand signals." He motioned to the dog and he sat. He motioned again and the dog laid down. He motioned again and the dog crawled across the floor. "This is only a small part of what he can do. He can walk across a limb six inches around. He can jump a six foot wall. He can alert you to danger with his growl. He attacks when you tell him. Gros Jacques watch," he said, and the dog came inches from my face snarling. "Gros Jacques quit," and the dog went over and sat by his side.

"I am very impressed, but I don't need a dog."

"I am sorry Mon Ami, but I must tell you I do not have your money. So it is the dog or nothing."

"I could take it out of your hide," I said.

"Yes, but it is only money, and like I said this dog will save your life. Is that worth any amount of money?" he said.

"No I guess not."

"His name is Gros Jacques."

"What is that in English?" I asked.

He thought for a second and said, "Big Jake."

It didn't look like I had any choice in the matter and I sort of liked the Frenchman even if he tried to cheat me. I agreed to the dog for the money and he shook my hand.

"I will miss Gros Jacque," he said, "he has kept me alive for some time." He put the dog on a leash and said, "Do not let him go until I am far away." He handed me another piece of leather. "This also is for the dog. It is a harness. A man can go many places where a dog cannot. This will make it easier to move him with you. I go now back to Canada. Do not let him go until I am gone for at least two days, he may follow me. I forgot to tell you he can trail with his nose very good. If you let him smell something and tell him to find it, he will find it. Now maybe you should go also. When they hear you got a dog for a thousand dollars it would not be so good for you. Look at me Mon Ami. Gros Jacque is one of a kind. There are no others like him. Take good care of him. I am gone."

He started to pack up and I left.

"Well Annie that is the story."

"Big Zach, you know you got the better of that deal."

"Yes," I laughed. "I didn't at the time, but I wouldn't trade Big Jake for all the money in Mr. Goldman's bank."

CHAPTER 31

"I have a big day tomorrow big Zach. I have to get word to the university about the statue and figure out how to get it to them and it is daunting. But my father is resting now, and I will too when the statue is in the museum."

We ordered room service and had a very nice meal. They cooked Big Jake's steak just the way he likes it, medium rare. After we ate we called it a night and Annie snuggled next to me until morning.

Annie spent the next day writing letters to the university so Big Jake and I went to see Efren.

"Efren," I called, "you here?"

Just then Sheba bounded around the corner and tackled Big Jake. They both took off running around the livery.

"Back here," Efren called. I walked back and Efren was just finishing up currying a horse. "Hey Big Zach," he said, "where's Annie?"

"She's busy writing letters today and getting caught up. I thought if you had some time I would go through some training with you and Sheba. She's at the age to start, and the sooner the easier it will be."

We spent the next several hours going over the things he needed to start with, and by the time I left, Sheba could sit, down, shake hands, come to him and speak.

"I can't believe she learned so fast," Efren commented.

"She's really smart and wants to please you," I said. "Always remember to keep it short and fun so she enjoys her lessons. Give it a week of going over these things she's learned and we'll add to it," I said. "I had better get back to Annie. See you in a few days Efren."

"Ok Big Zach, say 'hello' to Annie."

Big Jake and I left and walked back to the hotel. When we got to the room Annie was just finishing up her letters.

"How's it going?" I asked Annie.

"All done, just need to send them," she responded.

"Well get ready and well go to the post office and grab a bite to eat."

We went out and Annie posted her mail and we had lunch. So for the next week we relaxed and waited for Annie to get a response from her letters.

We were sitting in Annie's room when there was a knock on the door. Annie answered and a bellhop said, "This is for you ma'am," and handed her an envelope.

"Thank you," she said and handed him a nickel.

Annie came over and sat down. "It's the university's reply," she said opening the letter. For several minutes Annie read the letter. She looked up and I asked her what it said. She looked at me and said, "They are coming here."

"Who is coming here?" I asked.

"The President of the College and the Head of the Archaeology Department. They are really excited to see the statue and have something very important to tell me. They should be here with in the week."

"You know Annie, you can't tell these people the real story behind the statue. For one thing they wouldn't believe you, and for another it would probably label you a liar and a fraud. So you need to come up with a story they will believe and still keep it honest."

"Yes I know Big Zach, and I have been thinking of just that. I'm going to tell them very little and tell them I will write my paper and they can read about it. That way I can make sure the story is real and believable. They want me get them rooms here and set up a time to view the statue."

"There's another thing we need to address while we're at it," I said. "The map, it still contains three more sites and I think they all have something valuable there. Maybe you should make a copy of the map and we'll put the original in Mr. Goldman's vault."

"I was thinking the same thing," said Annie. "I should make it over and put my own clues to confuse and basically send whoever may find it on many a wild goose chase."

"Great idea Annie," I said, "and don't even tell me. I can always get to the real map, so what do you need to get started?"

"I'll make a list and go get what I need. On the way out I'll make reservations for the University President and the Head of the Archeology Department."

It took Annie nearly a week to finish the map. I was looking it over when a knock came to my door. I answered and a bellhop said, "This is for you," and handed me a note. I handed him a nickel and read the note. 'Big Zach I need to you as soon as you can come over, Mr. Goldman.'

I reread the note to Annie and said, "Since I have to go to the bank I'll take the original map and have him put it in his vault."

"Ok Big Zach," she said, "I'll put some finishing touches on this and see you later."

I left Big Jake with Annie and got a cab up to Mr. Goldman's bank.

CHAPTER 32

I went inside and Mr. Goldman was standing there. "Good of you to come, "he said. "I have important news for you. Come in my office."

I followed him in and sat down. "Well my boy I sent the gems to New York and just got word from my Broker. He estimates the value of all the gems at one point five million dollars. He says he will buy them from you for one point two million dollars, and after I take my commission you will have nine hundred and sixty thousand dollars split two ways. That's four hundred and eighty thousand dollars each for you and Annie."

"Do it," I said, "and invest mine any way you like."

"Well my boy, since I met you I have made a lot of money," Mr. Goldman said, "and from now on you can consider me your personal banker. If you need anything just let me know."

"What exactly does that mean?" I asked.

"It means my boy that if you are somewhere and need something, say some information on a piece of property or a person or are in trouble. Get me word and I will move the earth to help you."

"I appreciate that Mr. Goldman," I replied. "I have another request," I said. "Can I keep this package in your vault for safe keeping?"

"Yes, Big Zach. No problem."

"And one more thing, Annie has heard back from the university and they are coming down to see the statue. Can we use a room here next week to show it without anyone knowing what we're doing?"

"Sure you can, just let me know the time and I will have a room available for you." He stood and shook my hand.

I left and went back to the hotel.

I was a rich man, a very rich man but it didn't seem to matter. I was happy and had Annie and Big Jake. What else could a man want?

I opened my door to the hotel room and Big Jake greeted me with a wag and a bark. I petted him and went to look for Annie.

"Is that you Big Jake?" Annie asked.

"Yep it's me," I responded. I walked in and an older man was sitting with Annie.

He got up and put out his hand. "The names Marshall Jeffrey Kinkaid. Nice to meet you Big Zach. Let me get right to the point of my visit. We have a little girl lost in the woods, we have put out search parties but haven't been able find her. I was told you have a very good tracking dog. I wouldn't normally get mixed up in things like this but the little girl is the daughter of a very influential judge in the district. He would consider it a favor if you and your dog could help."

"Of course we'll help," I said. "How long has she been missing?"

"Two days now."

"Did she wonder off or was she taken?" I asked.

"The judge and his family were having a picnic down by the river off old Spring Road. The little girl went down by the river and when they called for her she didn't answer. They went to find her and she was gone."

"You know she could have fallen in the river and drowned," Annie gasped.

"Yes that occurred to me but we hope that isn't what happened to her."

"How old is she and what is her name?" I asked?

"Her name is Isabelle and she is eight years old," the Marshall answered.

"My first thoughts are being that her father is a judge. He may have enemies."

"We're checking into that right now but in the meantime can you help?"

"Yes of course we will," I answered. "Get me a piece of clothes she has recently worn and meet me at Efren's Livery in an hour. My horse is there and it isn't far from the road you mentioned."

I kissed Annie goodbye and she said, "I hope you find her Big Zach."

"I do to too," I replied and called Big Jake.

I got us a cab and a few minutes later we were at Efren's.

"Efren you here?" I called out.

"Yep, over here," he answered.

"I need you to saddle up Buck for me. A little girl is missing and the Marshall asked if Big Jake and I can help find her."

"Sure Big Zach, right away," he answered.

The Marshall and the other riders showed up a few minutes later and I followed them to the place the girl vanished.

CHAPTER 33

I told the Marshall and his men to stay put and let us see what we can find. I hefted Big Jake down and got the piece of clothing from the Marshall.

"Here Big Jake smell this." He took several smells and I told him to find. He put his nose down and scented all over the area and then he caught something and raced for the river. He scented around and went down river. He kept going quite a ways then he stopped and looked across the river. I went up to him and looked at the ground.

I motioned the Marshall over and said, "Did you see this?" pointing to the ground.

"No we didn't look this far down river."

"See the boot prints and the little foot prints? There was a struggle, she tried to get away. Looks like three different men. See the different boot prints? They had a boat and Big Jake's looking at the other side of the river. You know a quick way to get over there?" I asked.

"There's a ferry about five miles upriver," he responded.

I looked at the opposite side and said, "You know what's over there?"

"No, but I'll have one of my men stay here so we know we're in the right place."

We mounted up and road hard to the ferry. Once across we made our way down river.

"Marshall, there's Slim on the other side waving."

"Wave him over here," the Marshall said.

I told everyone to stay put again and gave Big Jake another smell from her clothes. He took a couple of whiffs and I told him to find. He went down to the river and scented around then took off up river. I told the Marshall to come with me and have his men follow with the horses.

Big Jake had the scent and he followed the river for about a mile and stopped, He looked my way and we caught up to him.

"Look," I said, "the same three boot tracks but no small, ones. They must be carrying her," I said out loud.

I told Big Jake to find again and he took off up the bank into some trees. We quickly mounted up and followed. Big Jake had the scent real good and he followed it until we came to a road. He scented around and took off up the road with us right behind. He followed the scent for several miles and his head made a sharp turn to the left back toward the water. He took off again and we followed. If it wasn't for the horses we would never had been able to keep up.

The trail led to some woods and Big Jake stopped his eyes glued to something up ahead. I motioned the riders to stop and stay put while I got down and made my way to Big Jake. I sighted down his nose and saw an old house with smoke coming out of the chimney. I grabbed Big Jake and found us some cover. I looked back at the Marshall and motioned him to come up real quiet like.

The Marshall came up to me and whispered, "What you got?"

I pointed to the shack and said, "She's in there."

"Let's move in real quiet," he said.

He gave the deputy's hand signals and we crept up on the house.

Luckily there was quite a bit of cover for us to hide in. When we got within twenty yards I whispered to him to stay down and I would see what I could find out. I told Big Jake to stay and made my way up to the side of the house. I crept up to a window and peeked in. The windows were really dirty but I could see three men and the little girl inside. I made my back to the Marshall.

"She's in there," I said. "I got an idea," I said to the Marshall. "I didn't see any guns but you can bet they have some. We have surprise on our side so this is what I think we should do. Get two of your men to watch the back door; if anyone comes out they can take them. We'll go through the front and take them by surprise. I know this is a risk but if we do this right we may not have to fire a single shot."

"Ok let's do it," the Marshall said.

I told Big Jake to follow and we snuck up to the house. The men at the rear signaled they were ready. I pulled both Colts and nodded to the Marshall. I kicked in the door and rushed in. One of the thugs went for a gun and Big Jake took him. One raised his hands while the third one went out the back door. I told Big Jake to quit and threw the man on the floor. The Marshall already had the other down and cuffed. I went to the little girl and she was crying holding her head in her hands.

I touched her and said, "It's alright Isabell your safe now."

She looked at me and said, "You know my name."

"Yes," I said, "your father sent us to help you."

"Oh, I knew he would mister. I was so scared."

"I know you were but you're safe now."

Big Jake came over to her and licked her face. "Gee mister what a pretty dog. Is he yours?" she asked.

"Yes, and his name is Big Jake."

"Thank you for coming for me. They said they would kill me if my father didn't do what they said."

"Don't thank us Isabelle," the Marshall said. "Big Jake there found you and led us right to you."

She hugged him and started to cry again. "I love you Big Jake," she said.

The Marshall and his men took the kidnappers into custody and Isabell rode with me and Big Jake back to town. When we arrived at the jail the Marshall sent one of his deputy's to fetch the judge. I handed down Isabell and let Big Jake off Buck.

"I trust you have this all in hand," I said to the Marshall. "me and Big Jake are going home."

I bent down and said goodbye to Isabelle and she said goodbye to Big Jake.

I heard her say, "I love you Big Jake," as we rode away.

I got back to Efren's about dark and told him what happened.

He said, "That Big Jake is something ain't he?"

"Yep," I said, and told Efren I'd see him later. I hailed a cab and went back to the hotel.

Annie was waiting when we got inside.

"What happened Big Zach, did you find the little girl?" she asked excitedly.

"Yes we did and she's just fine."

I told her the story and she got down and hugged Big Jake. "You're my hero," she said to Big Jake, "and I got room service coming with a big juicy steak."

He wagged his tail and kissed Annie on the face.

CHAPTER 34

The next morning there was a knock on the door. I answered it and the Marshall was there. I invited him in and he said he could only stay a minute.

"Turns out the judge was trying a case against a gangster here in town and he thought by taking his daughter the judge would let him go. He didn't know the judge very well. Even if something had happened to the girl he would have still done his job." He turned to leave and said, "I almost forgot the judge would like you, Big Jake and Miss Annie to come to his house this evening. That is if you not busy?"

I looked at Annie and she said, "We would be delighted."

He said, "The judge will send a carriage for you around seven."

"We'll be ready," Annie said.

The Marshall turned to leave and said, "And don't forget Big Jake. Isabell's request."

I nodded and he left.

We got all cleaned up and brushed out Big Jake.

"Big Jake," Anie said when she finished. "You are the most handsome dog in the world. You ready to see Isabelle?"

Big Jake barked and went to the door.

When we arrived at the judge's home. There were several other carriages parked outside. I helped Annie down and Big Jake followed us to the door.

"How do I look?" I said to Annie.

"You look just fine," she said straightening my tie.

The door opened and a maid ushered us in. Big Jake rushed over to Isabelle and licked her face. She hugged him and said, "See mommy I told you he was beautiful."

"Yes you were right, he is very handsome."

The judge introduced himself and his wife to us and then to the others in the room. I was totally surprised to see Mr. Goldman sitting in a chair. Now I knew how they knew about Big Jake. The Marshall was their too. Mr. Goldman got up and shook both our hands.

"So it was you who told the Marshall about Big Jake?" I said.

"Guilty as charged Big Zach. I'm so glad you could help. Isabelle means a great deal to us. She's my granddaughter."

I said, "I am too, she is a sweet girl who didn't need to endure such a fright."

"Mister Taylor," Isabelle said tugging on my sleeve. "Does Big Jake know any tricks?"

"Yes he does Isabelle," I replied. "He knows quite a few."

"Can you show me? Please, please."

I looked at the judge and he nodded it was ok.

I said, "Ok let's give him some room and I'll show you."

I had Big Jake sit-up, shake hands, speak, and lay down, play dead, rollover, wave goodbye and bow.

Isabelle screamed with joy. "He is so smart!" she said.

"Ok one last trick. Isabelle you stand in the center of the room and hold both your hands out." I told Big Jake to 'hup' and he jumped over her head and came back to her licking her face.

"Big Jake," she said, "you saved me from those bad men. I love you," and she cried.

Just then a maid came in and said, "Dinner is served."

I had Big Jake lay by me and Annie and we had a nice dinner with the judge and his family.

After dinner the judge pulled me over to the side and thanked me for saving his daughter's life.

I said, "I'm glad it all worked out. If you ever need anything let me know."

"My father told me you were a kind, decent man. It's my pleasure to have met you, Annie, and Big Jake."

"It was an honor to meet you and your family as well," I replied.

It was time to leave and we said our goodbyes. I had Big Jake wave goodbye to Isabelle and we went out to the carriage.

When we got back to the hotel I grabbed Annie and said, "How about some fun," and took her bed for the evening.

The week went by and the people from the university finally showed up. Annie met with them and said she would see them first thing in the morning and show them the statue. I sent a message to Mr. Goldman to see if eleven o'clock the next morning would be ok for the showing. I got a message back saying it was all set up.

The next morning Annie and I met the University President and his colleague in the lobby of the hotel. She introduced me to them.

"Mr. Addison this is Big Zach." I shook his hand, "And Mr. Preston, Big Zach." I shook his hand.

"It's nice to meet both of you," I said. "The meeting is all set up shall we go?"

"Yes," they both said, and we got a cab to Mr. Goldman's bank.

When we arrived at the bank Barney opened the door and Mr. Goldman was waiting in the lobby. Annie introduced them and Mr. Goldman said, "Right this way." He ushered us into a room and said his good byes.

There were two guards with guns outside the door. We went in and the bag the statue was in was sitting on a table. Annie went over and let the bag drop. Both men gasped.

"It is beautiful Mr. Addison," the University President said walking over to it. Mr. Preston walked over and produced a magnifying glass and spent a few minutes looking it over.

When he was done he said, "Magnificent work. It is definitely Anasazi. I can't wait to hear how you found this. May I lift it?" he asked, and Annie nodded to him.

He picked it up and sat it back down, "Must weigh twenty to twenty five pounds," he commented.

"What do you think it is worth?" Mr. Addison said.

"Worth," Mr. Preston said, "it's priceless! This will be our finest piece of Anasazi art in our museum.

Mr. Addison looked at me and said, "Can we have a minute alone with Miss. Stillwell?" I nodded to him and Annie and left the room calling Big Jake to come with me.

We went out the front door and found us place to wait.

CHAPTER 35

"Miss Stillwell," Mr. Addison said. "We are humbled that you chose our university to give this priceless piece of art to. We have been saddened for many years about your father's demise. He was one of our most respected professors."

Mr. Preston nodded in agreement. "May I Miss Stillwell?" and he pointed to the chairs. Annie sat down and didn't say anything.

"We have a proposition to make you," Mr. Preston said. "As you know I am currently the Head of Archeology at the University. I am taking another position Mr. Addison has given me and we now have an opening for a new head of the department. We are offering you this position. We have gone over your history with the university and it is impeccable. We are offering you a full Professorship with tenure. It comes with a nice salary, a house on the campus and all the respect that comes with this position. We also have been building a new wing to the museum. The chancellors and we have decided to name it after your father. It will be called, The Morgan Stillwell Memorial Wing. We would be honored if you would accept."

"Don't answer now," Mr. Addison said, "think about it and we can talk again tomorrow."

They all got up and looked at the statue. Mr. Addison said, "Magnificent," and they left the room.

When I saw them coming out I hailed a cab and we went back to hotel. We said our goodbyes to them and went to our rooms.

"Well?" I said, "I'm busting to know what they said."

Annie sat down and said, "This is all overwhelming. They offered me the position of Head of the Archeology Department, a full professorship with tenure, a house on the campus and a nice salary."

"Annie," I said, "how wonderful; the teaching position you've always wanted and more."

"Yes," she said stunned. "What I've always wanted."

"Why the gloom and doom?" I asked. "It's your dream come true."

"I know it is," said Annie. "But…"

"But what? I am so happy for you," I said with excitement.

She looked at me and said, "What about us Big Zach? I can't ask you to live in a lonely house until I get home every day. It would kill you and Big Jake."

"Look Annie," I said, "Chicago is not that far and we can come visit you."

She looked up at me with tears in her eyes. "I love you both so much," she said.

"And we love you too Annie. But we will not stand in your way. An opportunity like this comes once in a life time. You do want to teach don't you?" I asked.

"Yes, yes I do more than anything."

"Then it's settled, take the position and live out your dream."

"Are you sure Big Zach?" she asked.

"Yes I'm sure; and we couldn't live with each other knowing you passed this up. You would always wonder what if."

"I knew you would see it this way. I just had to be sure. I will take the position on one promise. You and Big Jake come and see me as often as you can."

"It's a deal Annie."

"What will you do now Big Zach?"

"Well I promised Efren I would help train Sheba. We have already started and she can sit, come, shake hands, speak and down."

"That's great Big Zach. Efren loves that dog so much."

"Don't you worry about us. We will be just fine."

"I can't believe all that's happened since you bumped into me on the street that day," Annie said. "I know it's hard to believe but it is something I will never forget."

"Me too," I said. I reached over and kissed Annie.

"What are we sitting here for? We have a celebration to start. Where would you like to go?"

"Anywhere you want," I said, "it's on me."

We hailed a cab and took Big Jake to Efren's for the evening, and celebrated until early in the morning.

The next day she met with Mr. Addison and Mr. Preston. She accepted the position and they made arrangements to have the statue moved to the museum. They both accompanied it all the way back.

Annie made arrangements to have her household goods moved to Chicago and three days later we said goodbye.

"I will miss you both so much," she said, tears in her eyes.

"We will miss you too Annie." Big Jake jumped up and licked her face.

"I love you both. Don't forget your promise Big Zach. Come see me when you can."

"We will Annie," I said and we kissed for the last time. "Annie," I said, "remember the surprise I had for you."

"Yes," she said, "I do."

"Have you checked your bank account lately?" I asked.

"No I haven't."

"Well the next time you do there will be considerable more money in it."

"How much more?" she asked.

"About four hundred and eighty thousand more," I said.

"Where did it come from?" Annie asked?

"Remember the gems around the statue in the cave?"

"Yes," she said.

"I just happen to take a few handfuls before I blew it up. Mr. Goldman sold them for us and put the money in your account."

"You, you wonderful man." I pulled the emerald from pocket and handed it to Annie. "It's beautiful," Annie said looking a little confused. "It's yours to do as you wish with. If you ever get into financial trouble you can sell it and buy yourself a small country." Annie laughed. "Take care Annie," I said and she left out of our lives.

I moved out of the hotel and back in to Efren's the next day. I stayed in St. Louis for over a year helping Efren train up Sheba and learning how to draw those Colts from my holsters. Sheba turned out to be quite the dog. She could do almost everything Big Jake could do, but she didn't hate Indians. Yet! By the end of the year I could draw and shoot pretty fast and hit what I aimed at.

I told Efren that it was time for me and Big Jake to leave; a wagon train full of prospectors bound for California was leaving in a few days and I thought we might tag along. Efren understood and said he would miss us. I told him I'd be back next year and to take good care of Sheba.

I was packed up ready to leave when a boy came to the livery. "Are you Big Zach?" he said.

"Yes," I said.

"Here," he said, "this telegram is for you."

I had never received a telegram before so I opened it and read it. It was from Mr. Addison the University President. It said that Annie was missing. She had gone home from school for the weekend and never arrived for classes the following Monday. They had been to her house and it was all tore up, and the police were investigating. He feared foul play. Her discovery of the statue had made all the newspapers, and he thought that maybe it has to do with that. As Annie had no one else he thought of me and wondered if I could help.

I was stunned and Efren just got mad.

"What are we going to do Big Zach? Annie needs our help."

"I know."

"You ain't leaving me out of this either, I'm going with you, no buts," Efren said.

"Ok, but what about your livery?"

"I can get someone to manage it while were gone."

"Ok Efren, we both go. I have to see a judge. Get your affairs in order and we'll leave as soon as we can."

EPILOG

I hailed a cab and told him to take me to the judge's house. I arrived and was told the judge was at the courthouse. I got back in the cab and he took us downtown to the courthouse. I walked in and Marshall Kincaid was there talking to some deputies. He walked over and shook my hand.

"Good to see you again Big Zach," he said. "You looked troubled, anything I can do?"

"Annie's been kidnapped."

"No," he said, "when?"

I showed him the telegram and he said it was out of his jurisdiction but that he had a good friend who ran the Chicago office.

"I could telegraph him and ask him to help you," he offered. "You are going to Chicago aren't you?" he asked.

"Yes," I said, "right away."

"I need to speak to the judge, can I see him?"

"Wait here and I'll see." He came back a few minute later and said, "He will see you."

I followed him to the judge's chamber and he knocked. A voice said to come in. I motioned for the Marshall to come in with me and he closed the door.

"Well Big Zach Taylor. How are you?" he said shaking my hand.

"I have a problem I hoped you could help with." I gave him the telegram and he read it.

"My," he said, "not Annie!"

"Yes," I said, "and she needs help."

"What can I help you with Big Zach? Ask me anything."

I told him, "I needed a marshal's badge."

They both looked at each other and then the judge spoke to Marshall Kincaid. "How can we get Big Zach a badge?" he said.

"I see why you think you may need it Big Zach, but are you sure about this?"

"Yes I may need to go places and see people, and the badge will give me the authority. People will have to talk to me. After all doesn't a Marshall have jurisdiction every place including the Indian nations?"

"Yes he does Big Zach." replied the Judge.

"I have an idea Judge," Marshall Kincaid said. "You can appoint him an Honorary Marshall and put him on the rolls. Honorary Marshalls don't get paid. But they still have all the authority. He can get into places he might not be able to otherwise. Besides, I have a friend who runs the Chicago office. I'll telegraph him and tell him he's coming up and lend him a hand with the investigation."

"Ok Big Zach," he said, "raise your right hand." The judge swore me in and handed me a badge. "If you need anything," the judge said, "telegraph me or the Marshall here and we'll help anyway we can." "Thanks to both of you," I said. "I'll tell Annie what you did for her."

"Find her Big Zach."

"I will," and I shook their hands.

The Marshall walked me out and said, "Good luck Big Zach, let us know if you find her."

"I will," and I left for Efren's.

"Oh by the way, my Marshall friend's name is Will Walker."

"I found someone to manage this place," Efren said. "So what's next?" "You still got the Walkers?" I said.

"Sure do," Efren said, "right here," and he lifted up his shirt showing off a pair of new holsters.

"Good," I said. "What about a riding sack for Sheba?"

"When I had the holsters made I had old Baxter make one for me."

"Then let's make a list of provisions and you go get them. I need to go to the bank and get the maps. We'll meet back here, load up and go."

"Ok big Zach," Efren said.

I walked out of Efren's livery and hailed a handsome cab to the bank. Mr. Goldman was in the bank and I told him what happened. He got the map and told me good luck.

"I hope you find Annie, we'll pray for her."

I headed back to Efren's and when I returned Efren was already loading the supplies.

"Did you get everything?" I asked.

"Yep," Efren said, "and another thing I thought we might need."

"What's that?" I asked.

"This here bow and plenty of arrows."

We loaded up and headed to Chicago to find Annie. Little did I know we would be looking for the: **Secret of the Aztec Pyramid.**

Made in the USA
San Bernardino, CA
05 August 2018